Citation
for
Murder

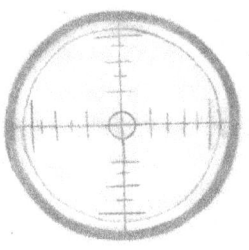

Look for other Western & Adventure novels by
Eric H. Heisner

Along to Presidio

West to Bravo

Seven Fingers a'Brazos

Above the Llano

T. H. Elkman

Mexico Sky

Short Western Tales: Friend of the Devil

Wings of the Pirate

Africa Tusk

Fire Angels

Cicada

Conch Republic, Island Stepping with Hemingway

Conch Republic - vol. 2, Errol Flynn's Treasure

Follow book releases and film productions at:
www.leandogproductions.com

Citation for *Murder*

Eric H. Heisner

Illustrations by Adeline Emmalei

Visit our website at
www.leandogproductions.com

Illustrations by: Adeline Emmalei

Dustcover jacket design: Dreamscape Cover Designs

Edited by: Story Perfect Editing Services – Tim Haughian

Hardcover ISBN: 978-1-956417-06-7

Printed in the United States of America

Dedication

*Los Angeles: a place where anyone
can find their people.*

Special Thanks

Amber Word Heisner, Tim Haughian,
&
Dan Farnam: For letting me sleep behind the couch.

Note from Author

Political correctness and comedy are often in opposition. Dark humor will step across that line to examine our world with a mirror held up to criticize society. Looking back now, the news events that occurred while I lived in Los Angeles are now thought to be bizarre or unbelievable. It was a very strange time of frequent freeway shootings and televised car chases; tabloid talk shows and reality television. As these incidents flooded the media, I was going to Hollywood parties with body-painted ladies and no-pants-half-hour. All while scraping together rent by delivering scripts for the star of *The Graduate*... You can't even imagine how many parking tickets I received running errands around Santa Monica!

Eccentric characters tend to wander to sunnier climates, and Southern California has more than its fair share of them. Here is a reluctant hero who makes his way through the urban jungle of LA, in a time of change when the news media creates a sense of fame, and the distinction between reality and fiction is molded through the lens of the camera.

Eric H. Heisner

September 9, 2022

Southern California: 1996

Chapter 1

Just a bright summer day on the city streets of Santa Monica... A chilly ocean breeze blows steadily, and the smell of saltwater gives that distinct scent of a beach community. Seen through a telescopic viewfinder, a *Meter Maid* - Parking Enforcement Officer, drives a three-wheeled patrol vehicle. He exits his official police cart on a car-lined street. The crosshairs of the long-range scope adjust for distance and then slowly moves along with the uniformed officer, as he walks around a parked car to inspect the time on the meter.

Standing before the lollipop-shaped parking apparatus, the Meter Maid gives the coin-filled head a few solid whacks, rattling the change inside. He then peeks at his pocket watch and steals a glance both ways down the empty sidewalk before taking out his ticketing machine. The crosshairs of the long-distance scope scan up the street and back again, as the parking enforcement officer punches in the vehicle's license plate information.

As the Meter Maid tears off a printed parking ticket, the sighted crosshairs of the scope jump slightly, followed by two muffled gunshots. Parking ticket still in hand, the Meter Maid folds to his knees and crumples into a lifeless heap beside the sidewalk. The sighted crosshairs linger as the breeze flutters the paper ticket, and everything is quiet.

After a short time, a solitary pedestrian walking a dog approaches to discover the Meter Maid laid out on the ground. The middle-aged woman stares down at the uniformed figure, and then glances around to find that she is alone on the street. She pulls the leash of her sniffing dog, as it starts to lift its leg to urinate on the body, and promptly leaves the crime scene. The scoped viewfinder follows the woman down the sidewalk, and then sweeps back to look at the expired Meter Maid with the undelivered citation.

~*~

The distinctive cross-haired view of a telephoto camera lens adjusts focus on the red brick wall of a private residence. The long-distance lens scans across the side of the house and through the neatly trimmed shrubbery, stopping at a window with a clear view of one of the house staff cleaning the parlor. The woman vacuuming the curtains is wearing the classic black and white *sexy maid* outfit that is often sold in costume shops.

The camera clicks-off several shots and then pans across the exterior of the home again to stop at a bedroom window. Inside, a woman walks out from a brightly lit bathroom, moves past the bed and fixes her hair in front of a full-length mirror. She adjusts her blouse over the straps of her bra and then goes to the house intercom by the door. She pushes the button and leans toward the speaker, her lips moving as she talks into the white box.

A minute later, the woman in the French maid outfit appears at the doorway with a smile, feather duster in hand. Feigning surprise, the woman backpedals across the room, falling onto the bed. The maid steps into the master bedroom, drops the duster to the floor and reaches behind her back.

Unexpectedly, the entire maid dress drops to the floor. Wearing only the hat, long stockings, and a grin, she advances toward the woman lying on the bed and climbs on top of her.

Citation for Murder

The camera shutter clicks, pauses, and then resumes clicking wildly as the crosshairs focus on the amorous couple.

"Got'cha... Finally caught her in the act..."

The camera's long, extended lens suddenly goes dark, until the elongated snout of a German Shepherd dog racks into focus through the viewfinder. Close... Very, very close... Filling the entire frame, the security dog peels back its lips and gives a low, rumbling growl, as a trickle of saliva drips from its barred canine teeth. The camera tentatively clicks-off several more shots, before pitching backward as the dog lunges.

~*~

A tree-lined street in a residential neighborhood of North Hollywood is filled with the sounds of nearby traffic and the chirping of birds. Vehicles are parked, bumper-to-bumper, all down the block. A damp, morning mist still lingers heavily in the air. A quirky man with a camera slung over one shoulder exits a two-story stucco apartment building, walks down the steps and proceeds to the line-up of cars.

Clive Wilts is small in stature with a paunchy bulge of unattended girth around his middle. He is outfitted in his standard uniform of tropical shirt worn under a sport jacket, complimented by jeans and a pair of scuffed-up boat shoes. Making his way down the line of parked cars, he stops at a 1987 cherry-red Fiero with custom T-tops. The small two-seater sports car is squeezed in at the end of the line of cars about twelve feet from a fire hydrant.

Sliding a jumbled wad of keys from his pocket, Clive abruptly clenches them in his fist, turning his knuckles white. A profane growl escapes from his lips, and his eyes narrow. Tucked under the wiper blade is a crisp, orange parking ticket, not yet damp from the morning dew. Clive snags the citation from his windshield and reads the hand-scribbled information on the back. *"Parked in a Red Zone… What the F#*%! Red Zone? This is total crap!"*

Walking around to the front of the car, he sees that his bumper is just barely hanging over the red-painted curb. Infuriated, he looks to the parking ticket again and goes into a fit of comic rage, mashing the slip of paper into a ball and throwing it as hard as he can. A breeze catches the wadded citation, mid-air, and blows it back, bouncing off his shoulder. A stream of unintelligible obscenities tumbles from his mouth, as if trying to utter every foul word that's ever been heard.

Finally getting a grip on himself, he peers down the street and, still red-faced with anger, heaves a deep breath. Clive kicks the wadded-up ticket which bounces off the door, hits the painted curb and then rolls beneath the parked vehicle. He squats down and gets on his knees to peer under the car. Letting out a grunt, Clive drops to his belly, scooching flat on the pavement to stretch far enough to grasp the crumpled paper with his fingertips.

Smoothing the citation out again over his bent knee, he looks down the car-lined street and places the wrinkled ticket back exactly where it was under his windshield wiper blade. He grumbles, "Screw them…" Satisfied, he nods to himself and walks to the neighborhood coffee shop around the corner and just down the street.

Chapter 2

Clive sits at one of the small tables inside the coffee shop with a drink and froufrou, display-case Danish. He slips his cellular telephone from his coat pocket and flips it open. The large, light-up display reads: *no messages; no signal*. "Stupid thing." He raises the phone up in the air and waves his arm around, trying to get a better signal. Without success, he eventually snaps it shut and drops it back into his pocket. After taking a bite of his pastry, he sips from his steaming coffee cup and watches the man at the next table reading the morning paper.

~*~

Chewing very, very slowly, Clive has another sip from his coffee and continues to watch the man with the newspaper. He takes the last morsel of his breakfast and murmurs under his breath, "Cripes! You read all the classified ads, too?" Disgruntled, he adds, "Maybe check out the article on *Get a Life* while you're at it." The man turns the last page, gives a shake to straighten the newspaper out, and Clive readies to spring for the daily once it has been abandoned. Leaving Clive's obvious intentions entirely unnoticed, the man, deep in concentration, continues to read at his leisure. Clive groans, "For heaven's sake...!" He digs out his phone again, flips it open and checks the display for a signal.

Noticing somebody passing by the front window outside on the sidewalk, Clive turns to observe as an attractive woman who frequents the coffee shop approaches the entrance.

Quickly adjusting himself, Clive speaks into the flipped-open cell phone, a bit too loud, in mock conversation. The woman enters and, on her way to the serving counter, makes a point of walking toward Clive. Smiling, she gives him a friendly wave. With a flirty sweep of her hair, she pauses at his table and asks, "Any big cases today?"

Keeping his cool, Clive nods and gives a playful wink. He points to the mobile phone at his ear and silently mouths, *I'm on one now.* Surprisingly, she appears impressed and lingers a moment to casually observe him. Clive notices her listening and sputters into the phone. "Uh, huh... Yeah, I know that. Okay... I'll have him by this afternoon." He glances up to see that he still has her attention, so he continues the charade. "Yeah, sure... No, I won't need any police backup on this one. I can manage him myself... Yeah, I'll handle it *my* way."

Still smiling, the woman finally turns away and goes to the coffee counter to place her order. Clive watches her, snaps the cell phone closed and sets it on the table, next to his coffee. He looks to the table opposite, where the man was reading, and sees only the folded newspaper left behind. About to make his move, another customer casually walks by and lifts the unattended daily paper from the table. Halfway out of his seat, Clive almost says something to claim it, but keeps silent when he notices the woman is still watching. Quickly composing himself, he forces a smile in her direction, which she returns sincerely.

Clive gathers up his cell phone and nearly empty cup, preparing to leave. He ambles to the front of the coffee shop and, as he pushes the door open, a cute voice calls from behind, "Go get 'em, Magnum!" Clive turns back to see her grinning, gives an awkward wave, bumps into the frame of the door, and then shuffles outside.

~*~

Citation for Murder

Turning the corner onto his street, Clive notices the whole side of the block is clear, except for his car at the end. Hearing the distant rumbling sound of a city street-sweeper, Clive looks to a no-parking sign displaying the days for street cleaning. "Oh, shit!!!"

Digging his wad of keys out from his pants pocket, Clive runs to his car. Frantically, he fumbles with them, as he looks over his shoulder while trying to put the key in the door lock. Finally, he unlocks the door, pulls it open and jumps into the driver's seat. He puts the key in the ignition, turns it to start the engine, and looks up to see multiple parking citations tucked under his windshield wiper. Both hands reach up to grip the steering wheel, and he shakes it maniacally. "ARRGH... @#%! ... *%#@! ..."

~*~

The sporty, red Fiero swings into a small parking lot adjacent to a rundown, Spanish adobe-styled office building. Clive gets out and goes around to the front of the complex. Strolling down the sidewalk, he notices a three-wheeled parking enforcement cart idling directly behind a white, Mazda Protégé with a Meter Maid sitting patiently inside.

Clive walks past the vehicles and sees the arrow on the space's meter only having about two more minutes remaining. He looks back at the lurking Meter Maid, with the ticket book at the ready, and gets a queasy feeling down in his gut. Reaching into his pants pocket, he takes out a quarter and slips it into the nearly expired meter.

The Meter Maid promptly hops from the tiny cart, rushes up to Clive and barks, "Hey you...! Is this your car?" Clive rubs his hands around and over the head of the meter, and then bends down to peek underneath it. He glances at the parking official and mutters aloud, "Huh... What the heck...? Where did my gumballs go?"

7

"It's illegal to feed someone else's parking meter."

Clive turns around to face the upset Meter Maid, putting on an innocent expression. "Hey, did you see that? What a gyp! I put my money in there."

"I know you did. You can't do that!"

"What a rip-off..." Clive rocks back on his heels, turns and struts over to pull open the front door of the office building. Still fuming, the Meter Maid calls after Clive. "Hey, buddy... Don't you ever do that again! Got it...? You understand me...?" When Clive waves dismissively over his shoulder, the parking attendant exclaims, "Next time, I'll have you arrested!"

Clive reaches into his front pants pockets, feels around contemptuously and then puts a satisfied look on his face. "There are my gumballs..." As he goes inside, he turns to smile at the Meter Maid, calling out, "Have a nice day!"

Chapter 3

Inside the building, Clive climbs up a worn, marble staircase to the second floor. He strolls down the empty hallway, stops at the last door on the left and faces the painted glass window which reads:

Clive Wilts Detective Agency
~ Licensed, Private Investigator ~

Entering the detective agency, Clive closes the door softly behind him and looks around the vacant reception area. Along one side of the room, a lone desk with an aged-yellow computer sits surrounded by stacks of files, red-notice unpaid bills and several empty coffee mugs. Three vinyl-covered, padded chairs that look as if they were salvaged from a liquidated doctor's office are opposite the desk. Clive strolls to the back of the room and faces a frosted-glass door with bold letters painted on it:

Detective Wilts, P. I.

Clive enters his private office and flips on the light. Hanging on the cracked, plaster walls are vintage newspaper clippings displayed in cheap, black plastic document frames. The different newspapers with similar photos are all about the same subject matter. A few of the front-page headlines display a hero headshot of Clive from more than a decade ago.

Moving around his desk to the windows, Clive sniffs something in the air and flinches in revolt. "What is that smell?" He peers into the trashcan, gives it a nudge and waves his hand. Standing at the wall of windows, he pulls up the shades and cranks the old, paint-crusted handle to open the casement. Tentatively he sniffs the air again and shudders before calling, "Delores… DELORES!!!"

Clive takes off his sport coat and tosses it onto a worn-out, leather couch before plopping down in the tufted chair at his desk. Rocking back in his executive throne, he hears the glass rattle on the office front entry door and then hears it close. After listening a moment, Clive curiously calls out, "Delores…?"

When no audible reply is heard, Clive leans forward, trying to peer through his half-closed doorway. A shadow passes by the frosted, glass-panel door and it swings open to reveal a slightly attractive young lady in a librarian-type outfit. She smiles courteously when she sees Clive and remarks, "Good morning, Mister Wilts. How was your long weekend in Palm Springs?"

With an expressive show of coolness, the investigator leans back in his chair to stare at the chipped plaster ceiling. "Fine… *If* you consider crawling through cactus and desert scrub, then hiding in the bushes for seventy-two hours straight in 100-degree heat okay…"

"Any interesting adventures?"

Clive turns his gaze to her at the doorway and smirks. "Just one friendly dog…"

"Was it a big one?"

Clive nods and taps his index finger on his desktop. "Yeah… Luckily for me, the fence *wasn't*, though." He leans way back in his creaking chair and digs into his pants pocket. Pulling out a roll of 35mm film, he pitches it to the assistant, who catches it mid-air like a seasoned pro. Scooting his chair up to his desk, Clive puts on his best Bogart impersonation. "Hey, Shweetie... Could ya take dat to *Prints 'R Us* and have it ready for our client dis afternoon?"

"Special package...?"

"Yeah... Enlargements, and all da trimmings..."

Delores smiles, as she caresses the small, round canister of unprocessed film. "Did you get her this time?"

Clive smiles confidently and replies in his usual voice. "I'm back, aren't I?" Spinning his chair, he looks out the window and down the busy street. "Anything happen around here this weekend?"

"I went to a baseball game at Dodgers Stadium."

"Yeah? How was it?"

"It was a good time."

Clive turns his chair and reminisces. "The last time I went to a ballgame, I was on a date with a woman."

The news of her boss on a romantic outing is out of place and arouses her interest. "Yeah? How did it go?"

With a grin, Clive jokingly replies, "I kissed her on the strikes, and she kissed me on the balls." The jest takes a moment to sink in, and Delores shakes her head without comment. Sunlight beams in through the windows, and she reaches over to flip off the switch to the overhead lights. Clive scoots his chair forward and nods. "Good to save on electricity..."

She continues his statement, "...before they turn it off."

He grimaces, looks to the messy stack of papers on his desk and then turns his chair to look out the windows again. "Anything else happening?"

"Another Parking Enforcement Officer was shot down in Santa Monica."

Somewhat interested, Clive half looks over his shoulder. "You mean a Meter Maid?"

"I don't think they call them that anymore."

"Why not?"

Delores shrugs and leans on the frame of the door. "What do you call the guy ones then?"

"Heck, I call 'em Meter Maids. If they want to take the jobs away from working women, I don't think they should get a special title for it." He thinks on it a quick moment and adds, "That goes for airplane stewardesses, too!"

Delores rolls her eyes at her boss' curmudgeonly humor and tosses the film canister in the air a few times. "Well, I guess that's about it."

"Alright, give Mr. Goldleffer a call and make an appointment to have him come to the office this afternoon to see those photographs." He sniffs the air again and winces. "Get some air deodorizer for this place, too. It smells like something died in here." Affirming with a nod, the secretary steps through the entryway and begins to pull the office door shut behind her. Clive suddenly calls out, "Hold on! Wait a sec. What did you mean that *another* Meter Maid was shot?"

Pushing the door open again, Delores steps back inside. "You know, along with those two that were shot on Friday..."

Clive swivels his chair around and bangs his knee against the side of the desk. "Ow!!! What!? They were killed? Three of them? Where???"

"It's *all* over the news... Where have you been?"

With a scolding look, Clive gazes up at Delores, as he rubs his sore knee. "Out camping!"

She nods apologetically. "Well so far, two were shot in Santa Monica on Friday afternoon, and then another one near Beverly Hills yesterday."

"Really? The same shooter?"

"They don't know for sure, but they're thinking it was. They're not saying what type of gunshot it was yesterday."

His mind reeling, Clive asks, "How did they do it?"

"The first one on Friday was a close-range pistol shot. They said the second was a rifle from a long distance."

"A sniper shot, huh?" Clive reaches across his desk for the television remote and clicks it on. He scans the channels to get to a local LA newscast. Without taking his gaze from the television set, he asks, "Do they have any suspects?"

Delores rolls the film canister between her palms and shakes her head. "Nope... Nothing yet..."

Suddenly, she looks at Clive with pseudo-suspicion. "And, exactly where were *you* this weekend?"

Turning to her with a coquettish expression, Clive replies, "No, Delores, I was not out sport-hunting Meter Maids. Drop that film off. And, could you please grab me a newspaper, as well?"

"I'm all out of petty cash. Oh, and they said they're going to shut off the phones this week if we don't pay the overdue balance, too."

Using the remote control to flip through different news channels, Clive doesn't appear to be listening to her. "See if you can get your hands one a free one. An old yesterday's paper would be fine. Or, even one from Saturday..." Delores nods dutifully and steps out of the private office, closing the door behind her. The channels continue to flutter past, until Clive finds one that is covering the recent shootings.

Chapter 4

The sporty Fiero cruises down the streets of Santa Monica with the T-tops off and loud music playing. Stopping at a red light, Clive runs his fingers through his thinning hair and then reaches under the driver's seat to grab a canvas bucket hat. With his bright Hawaiian shirt, sport coat and droopy hat, he has the look of a pudgier version of Hunter S. Thompson.

Several blocks of traffic lights and bumper-to-bumper traffic later, he swings the sports car into the parking lot of the Santa Monica Police Station. He parks at the front in a space designated for on-duty officers. Glancing at the parked squad cars on either side, Clive is content with his own vehicle sitting low and nearly out of sight. The car door opens wide, and he rolls out, tosses his hat to the passenger seat and swings the door closed, not bothering to lock it.

Entering the lobby of the station like he owns the place, Clive strolls to the front counter and greets the receptionist. "Hiya, Shannequa... Is ol' Detective Buckley around today?"

Behind the partition, wearing a form-fitting police uniform, the eye-catching, extremely tall, dark-skinned woman smiles as he approaches. She taps her long, curved fingernails on the countertop and responds coolly. "It's been a long time, Clive-baby. What sort of *private dick* activities are you up to?"

Putting an elbow to the counter, Clive leans way in and gives his best puppy-dog eyes to the much taller woman.

Eric H. Heisner

"Honey, I'm looking to get lunch with Buckley and catch up. Then, if I'm lucky, maybe some dinner and dessert with you?"

Her bright smile widens, and she gives her whole body a quiver. "Ohhh, you're such a *naughty* little man… Stay here, I'll check." As she steps away, Clive scans the lobby of the police station, noticing the lack of activity.

There is a throat-clearing cough from down the hall, and Clive turns to see Shannequa curl a long fingernail at him to follow her. He mimics the cough, as if embarrassed, and sputters, "I really don't have the time for that now, Sweetie."

She shakes her head with a smile and slaps her open palm against her curved hip. "Get your little ass over here, Clivey. He said he would talk with you in his office." Clive jogs the short distance down the hallway and slips past the leggy desk officer. She peers down her nose at him and laughs. "You'd better hurry before he changes his mind."

Over his shoulder, he looks back at her and grins. "Dinner tonight?"

The well-built woman smiles and gives her ample breasts a two-handed boost. "You wish, little man!" Clive trips and catches himself just at Buckley's office door.

Inside the police detective's office, Buckley sits behind his desk playing a game of casino solitaire on his computer. When Clive knocks softly, Buckley clicks the mouse, and an official-looking police document pops up to block the screen. He looks across the stacks of files and then waves Clive in. "Yeah! Come on in." The private investigator pokes his head inside, looks around and grins. Buckley pushes back in his chair and grunts, "What do you want this time, Clive?"

After slipping inside and swinging the door closed behind him, Clive takes a seat. "How've you been, Buckley?" He sits to the front edge of the chair and leans forward to scan the items on the officer's desk. "Long time, no see, eh buddy?"

16

"I haven't seen *you* around, so things ain't been bad."

Not the least bit fazed by the insulting remark, Clive nods and fiddles with the pencil holder on the corner of the desk. "Yeah, thanks... I've been doing pretty good, too."

Buckley takes the pencil holder and moves it away to the other side. "Clive, I didn't ask."

Coyly, Clive's gaze flutters up to the man behind the desk. "But, I bet you were curious..."

The police detective shakes his head with disgust and groans, "Okay, out with it."

"Are you still sore at me?"

"I can't imagine why..."

Defensive, Clive puts on a decent display of innocence. "You would've done the same thing, too, if you were there. And, I told you I'd buy you a new boat."

Buckley pushes back in his chair and crosses his arms. "What do you want, Clive?"

Clive adjusts the collar of the Hawaiian shirt under his sport coat and absentmindedly glances around the room. Almost as an afterthought, he asks, "What's been going on around here lately? You catch that shooter yet?"

Surprised, Buckley snorts and answers, "Wow! It took you this long to show up and ask?"

"I was out of town on a case all weekend."

"Insurance fraud?"

"Messy divorce."

Buckley shakes his head, leans forward, and places his palms flat on his desktop. "Can't do it."

"Come on... I need the work, and you need some help. You don't even have to give me the credit for the nab, unless I go it alone without any police backup."

"No good... We have several detectives on it now."

Clive raises an eyebrow questioningly. "Several, huh? Don't you go all out on cop-killers?"

Buckley shakes his head again and lowers his voice. "Parking Enforcement Officers are *not* cops."

"They wear badges."

"So does Walmart security." Clive leans forward a bit more and tries to peek around to Buckley's computer screen. Annoyed, the detective turns it away. "Is there anything else I can help you with today, Mister Wilts?"

Clive rolls his eyes and grimaces at the proper name address from an old friend. "So, you're not bringing in any outside help?"

"Not on this one... Standard rate for a tip that follows through and brings the perpetrator in..."

"Shit, that's not even enough to pay for the parking tickets I got so far today!"

Sitting back in his chair, crossing his hands on his lap, Buckley shrugs his shoulders and fakes a grin. "Sorry, Clive... I'll be sure to let you know of any other cases down the line."

Slapping his knees before standing, Clive leans closer to Buckley and whispers, "Any suspects?"

The police detective rolls his eyes back, and then nods. "Yeah, we've narrowed it down to four or five thousand people in Santa Monica that don't like Meter Maids."

"You still call 'em that?"

"Not officially..."

Clive takes a step back and then opens the office door. "Thanks anyway. Sorry about what happened to your boat."

Buckley turns his head and looks back to his computer again. He stares at the screen a minute, until he realizes that Clive is still standing in the doorway. Looking up at the private investigator, he brusquely asks, "Is there something else?"

Clive smiles and glances down the uncrowded hall. "Did you want the door open or closed?"

"Open is fine."

Clive gives a friendly wave, pats his hand on the door frame and steps away. "See ya, pal. Don't be a stranger!"

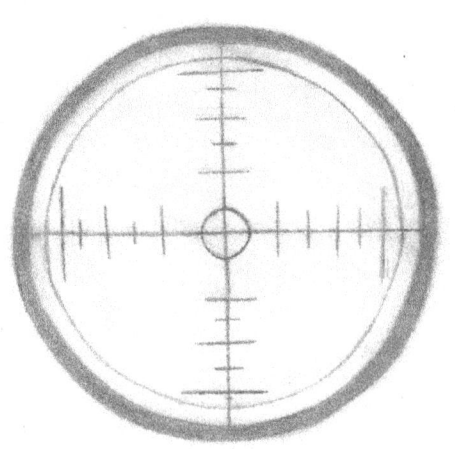

Chapter 5

Stuck in heavy traffic, the little red Fiero slowly creeps along Santa Monica Boulevard. Clive is distracted by the newspaper spread open on his lap, and he sneaks peeks at it between rolling stops. After taking a pen from the glove compartment, he circles the address of the first shooting and looks up at the sign to see the name of the cross streets. The light turns green, but the cars don't advance. Cranking the wheel, Clive hits the gas and zips down a side street.

~*~

On a palm-lined, neighborhood street in Santa Monica, Clive parks his car in a fire zone at the site of the first incident. A car-width away from the red-painted curb, a dark stain on the pavement is still apparent despite the wet trails of a city street-sweeper. Looking down the block at bumper-to-bumper parked cars and corresponding parking meters, Clive tries to picture the scenario in his mind.

Behind, in the distance, a parking enforcement cart with a flashing rooftop light is turning the corner. Staying close along the line of parked cars, the stealthy, three-wheeled vehicle comes steadily nearer, like a hungry shark on the prowl. Clive sits in his car, oblivious to everything around him but the blemish on the pavement. Suddenly, in his side-view mirror, he catches a glimpse of the Meter Maid only a car-length back.

Immediately, he slams his car into gear and cranks the steering wheel. Stepping on the gas, he peels away, leaving the parking enforcement vehicle in a cloud of burnt-tire smoke.

~*~

As Delores clicks away at her computer, an elderly gentleman sits in the waiting room of the Clive Wilts Detective Agency. H.W. Goldleffer, one of their few clients, sports a high-dollar wardrobe more than a few decades out-of-date. Irritated, the old man shifts in his seat and clears his throat. "Mademoiselle, could you please try phoning him once again? Today, I have multiple doctor appointments and a meeting with the divorce attorney."

Trying to appease the client, Delores picks up the phone and taps in a sequence of numbers on the push-button keypad. A moment later, they hear a phone ringing in the hallway. Delores and Mr. Goldleffer watch as Clive enters the office, fumbles in his pocket, and answers his cell phone.

Clive's eyes dart around the office, and he waves at his client, before feigning a conversation on the cellular phone. "Yeah, yeah, sure... I'm on it..." He holds his hand over the speaker of the flipped open phone and hurriedly shuffles past his elderly client and toward his private office. "I'll be with you in just a moment, Mr. Goldleffer. This is a very important call that I have to take." Ducking into his office and closing the door behind him, Clive puts the phone to his ear again and utters, "Hello?"

"Mr. Wilts, it's me."

"Delores?" Clive takes the mobile phone away from his face to see the caller identification and puts it to his ear again. "What do you need?"

"I've been trying to contact you for well over an hour. Mr. Goldleffer is here and is getting somewhat impatient."

Clive pauses to stare at the glass panel office door, realizing he can hear Delores at her desk very clearly. "Dammit! This stupid mobile phone only gets a decent signal when I'm two feet from my own office."

"Do you want me to send him in?"

Stepping across the room to the bank of windows, Clive looks outside to the line of parked cars down on the street. "Uh... Tell him you couldn't get through to me because of other important calls I'm taking."

"I think he can hear me."

Clive closes his flip-phone and tosses it on the desktop. He turns from the windows to the entry and raises his voice. "Hell, *I* can hear you! Send him in." He plops into his chair, pivots to the door, and it opens to reveal the waiting client. "Come on in Mr. Goldleffer, have a seat. I'm sorry about that... I was expecting another call."

The older gentleman steps in and sits in a chair across from Clive's desk. He places his walking cane across his knees, stares directly at the private detective and queries, "Soo...?"

Clive raises an eyebrow questioningly and replies, "Huh?"

Attempting to keep control of his growing annoyance, Goldleffer clears phlegm from his throat and then expounds. "Did you, or did you not, get the photographs?"

"Oh, yes..." Clive leans over and calls toward the partly open office door. "Delores, could you please get me the Goldleffer case file?"

Promptly, the receptionist appears at the doorway with the file folder already in hand. "Here it is, Mister Wilts. Anything else?"

Clive looks across his desk at the elderly gentleman. "Coffee, Mr. Goldleffer? Perhaps a nice cool glass of water?"

Impatiently, the old man waves away any further pleasantries. He grumbles, "No, no… Please, can I see the photos?"

Delores brings the folder with the pictures to the desk and Clive takes it with a smile. "Everything turn out okay?"

The receptionist nods, enlarging her eyes in an obvious way. "Yes, it's all there."

Clive acknowledges her look and places the folder on the desk. "That will be all for now." Delores exits the room and, with a quiet click, closes the door.

Leaning forward toward the desk, the older gentleman peers at the file folder under Clive's hand. "Could I see them now, Mr. Wilts?"

Clive opens the folder and prudently thumbs through the explicit photographs. He gets to one of the enlargements and studiously gazes at it. An impatient cough from the client gets his attention, and he shuffles the prints back into a pile. Holding the stack of photos, Clive looks earnestly at his client. "Now, I want to prepare you for what you will see. Realize, these matters can be very disturbing and emotional…"

"Oh, piss on all that bull-pucky! It had better be good! My lawyer said the dirt had to be one hundred percent to get the little tramp off my back without giving her a dime." Grimacing, Clive takes a deep breath and gingerly hands the stack of photographs over. The old man grabs and hastily flips through them.

Clive watches the elderly gentleman make his way though the pile with a stone-like expression. "If you need to talk about some of your feelings on the matter, I am here for you." The private detective shifts in his seat, waiting for a reaction. "Some folks get very upset when they see such infidelity. They act out of character in the oddest ways and do rash things." Clive watches as Goldleffer lets out whimpers of glee, as he scans through the photos again. "I understand it can be very upsetting. Everyone reacts to it differently."

Mr. Goldleffer suddenly looks up to Clive and flashes a yellow-toothed grin. "These are most exceptional! Excellent job, young man... That little hussy won't get a red cent!"

Clive, wide-eyed, is stunned at the man's enthusiasm. He offers a smile. "Well, sir... I'm happy to be of service. Another satisfied customer." Sighing with relief, Clive turns to glance out the window. "Looks like you won't be going out and 'pulling a crazy' like that Meter Maid fellow."

The elderly gentleman uses his cane to slowly stand, and then tucks the photos under his arm. His animated features go from giddiness to displeasure. "Meter Maids? I hate 'em all!!!" He spits to the side, and Clive leans forward to see the spray of spittle on the floor. "They're civets. Those useless pieces of sub-human garbage...!" Clive glances at the folder on his desk, smoothes his hand over the cover and looks up, as the old man continues his rant. "There are damned too many out there! They could use a good culling!"

Clive's jaw drops at the old man's outburst and inquires, "*Civets*...? What's a civet?"

Livid, Mr. Goldleffer ignores the question and declares, "My soon to be *ex*-wife is a filthy-tramp and a leech, but she's considerably higher on the lower ranks of society than a good-for-nothing, useless waste of a meaningless life, *Meter Maid!*"

Not believing what he is hearing, Clive shakes his head, gulps and mutters, "Okayyy... Get any parking tickets lately?" The private investigator stands and moves around his desk to escort Mr. Goldleffer out, before he has to hear more of his harsh opinions. As he is ushered out, the old man grumbles, "Having to pay to park your car...? Not in my day, ya didn't! They call this a free country. Hah! Except if you need to leave your car for a minute or two. To pay a meter is total horseshit! When I was a kid…"

"I'm so glad you're satisfied with the photographs of your soon-to-be ex-wife. Please pay Delores on your way out. Cash is fine." After gently pushing the older gentleman into the outer reception area, Clive closes his door firmly. He listens a moment as the client pays Delores while continuing his indignant tirade. A whistle of relief finally escapes Clive's lips, and he moves to his couch to lie down. Tucking his hands behind his head, his tired gaze scans the wall of framed newspaper clippings. Slowly, his eyes flutter shut, followed by a soft snore.

Chapter 6

Face down on the leather couch, Clive lies sleeping with a glistening stream of drool falling from the corner of his mouth. Dreaming, he imagines himself on a beach in a pair of skimpy, lifeguard swim-trunks and sporting a pair of *Top Gun* shades. Striking a hero pose, he watches the woman from the coffee shop run toward him as a wave rolls in and crashes at her feet. Splashing through the water, she jogs closer. Clive takes off his sunglasses, slings them aside and waits for her to run into his arms. Suddenly, she calls out, "Mr. Wilts... Mister Wilts?"

With a deep snort and a loud slurping of saliva, Clive, back on his leather couch, jumps up to a sitting position. Opening his eyes, he focuses to see Delores looking at him oddly from a few feet away. "Did I startle you, Mr. Wilts...?"

"No... What is it? What's going on?"

While sliding a pen into her hair bun, the receptionist straightens up and takes a few steps back. She gestures to the television, which has the sound muted. "Sorry to wake you..."

"I was just, uh, resting my eyes..."

Unconcerned, Delores shrugs and replies, "I thought you'd like to know."

Clive, half asleep, blinks his eyes as he tries to wake up. "Yes, I would... Know *what*...?"

"It's on the news. Another two Parking Enforcement, uh, Meter Maids, were killed today."

"Two? *Where?*"

"In Santa Monica again…"

Finally awake, Clive shakes his head in disbelief. "Really…? That's crazy…"

"The media is all over it." Delores turns to the television, points the remote, and clicks the mute button off. "People are in the streets cheering."

"Wow, that's *really* crazy."

She turns up the volume. "I can't believe it, myself."

The TV news personality moves aside for footage of dozens of people in the streets around the Santa Monica Promenade. The cameraman follows the on-scene reporter, who selects a citizen from the celebratory crowd. The reporter inquires, "Why are all these people cheering?" and holds his microphone out.

The young man looks around at the masses and shrugs. "It seems sick, but they're applauding that psycho that's been picking off the parking ticket guys."

With the crowd positioned behind him, the reporter steps directly in front of the camera and addresses the situation. "That's right… Not more than an hour ago, here in the coastal California city of Santa Monica, another Parking Enforcement Officer was gunned down in the line of duty, followed by another one, only half an hour later." The reporter turns to show his profile and offers the microphone to the man again. "How do you, as a law-abiding, private citizen of Santa Monica, feel about this?"

As the shouting continues behind them, the man replies with a grin. "Well, to tell the truth, I don't feel too bad about it."

Feigning horrific shock, the news reporter turns to face the camera lens and retorts, "Two officers in your community shot down while exercising their duty, and you don't feel any sort of remorse?"

The man shrugs indifferently and looks around at the crowd of rejoicing people. "It's not like they're *real* police, whose job it is to protect us or anything. In my neighborhood, they practically stalk your car to find some tiny thing to ticket. Meter Maids are a drain on society!"

Doubling down on his expression of shock, the reporter stands directly in front of the camera to address his audience. "Are Parking Enforcement Officers not real Police Officers??" The man pokes his head into the view of the camera to ask, "Hey, I just thought of something... What do you call the guy Meter Maids? *Meter-men*, like mermaids and mermen?"

The reporter looks at the man with mock concern, nudges him aside to get him out of frame and turns back to face the camera. Holding his look of disbelief, the reporter finishes his segment. "And there you have it. Callous disregard for authority, and unruly citizens cheering on an assassin..."

Clive stands up from the couch and takes the television remote from Delores. He changes the channel and finds another news crew on-location in Santa Monica. The camera pans several expired parking meters with cars sitting alongside, unmolested. The news commentator voices over the images. "There is anarchy in the streets, as local citizens are parking their cars and not paying the meters. It has become a carpark *free-for-all*, as many of the public servants who write the tickets have been calling in sick or not showing up for work at all."

Having heard enough, Clive lowers the volume and sits back down on the couch. "This is completely bonkers!"

Delores walks to the entry. "I thought it would interest you." She pulls the door closed behind her, and Clive looks up at the television again to see muted images of expired parking meters and cheering crowds waving orange parking citations.

Chapter 7

Clive drives through his neighborhood, past lines of parked cars, looking for any potential opening that is available. He cruises by several open gaps that are too small, even for his little two-seater. Stopping the car alongside a space where the curb is painted red for no apparent reason, he stares longingly. Looking around, checking his mirrors and over his shoulder, he mutters, "Too bad the shooter isn't in North Hollywood..." Wincing at the terrible thought, he continues searching the street for someplace to park. Circling the block, he approaches his apartment building again and stops to wait, as a car pulls out of a primo spot right in front.

~*~

After entering his apartment, Clive fastens the three locks on the door behind him. Walking through the kitchen, he tosses his sport coat over the back of a chair and steps to the window. He stands with the glow of neon upon him and looks out at the large number of people coming and going from the rear entrance of the neighborhood bar.

When he takes a step over to pull the refrigerator door open, the interior light clicks on to brighten the whole kitchen. Clive scans its meager contents of milk, cheese, beer and leftover spaghetti. He grabs a gold-colored can of Michelob from the middle shelf and lets the fridge door swing closed. Darkness consumes the kitchen again.

Moving through the small, one bedroom apartment, which is remarkably bare of furnishings, Clive passes a few yellowed newspaper clippings thumb-tacked to the bare walls. He switches-on the table lamp next to the couch and pushes a pile of clothes aside before plopping down. Staring across the room, he considers turning on his old television set which is built into its own cabinet.

Pulling the tab, Clive cracks the beer can open and takes a long swallow. He sits back deeper into the couch, rests his head and looks up to the slow-turning ceiling fan. Breathing deep, his eyes flutter closed for a moment and then reopen. After taking another sip of his beer, he reaches out and places it on the side table. He is about to drift off to sleep, when he hears a loud knock on his kitchen door.

Startled awake by the unexpected visitor, Clive sits up and looks around the dimly lit room. "Who the heck is that?" He picks up his beer, takes another quick swallow and checks his wristwatch for the time. Surprised at the late hour, he clears his throat and then yells toward the kitchen door. "Who is it?" There is a muffled, unintelligible response from the hallway. Clive shakes his head and, with beer in hand, ambles through the kitchen to answer the door.

Squinting through the door's peephole, Clive sees a nice-looking lady. Surprised by a female visitor at this hour, he sets his beer down and smooths his thinning hair in the reflection of the peephole. After a breath-check into his palm, he shrugs, satisfied. Clive unlocks the chain and dead bolts before cracking the door open. "Hello? Can I help you?"

The woman replies, "Yes… Is Detective Wilts here?"

Clive peeks down the hall both ways to see if she is alone. "What do you want with him?"

"Hello, my name is Catherine, and I am in desperate need of his help."

Opening the door a bit wider, Clive pokes his head all the way outside to get a better look. "In desperate need...? From here, you don't *look* to be in need of any help."

"I really *must* talk with Mister Wilts. Is he here?"

Clive opens the door all the way and gives her a look. "I'm Detective Wilts... How can I be of service to you?" Catherine uses the opportunity to slip past him and then anxiously waits for Clive to close the kitchen door behind her. Taken off-guard by the aggressiveness of inviting herself in, Clive feebly mutters, "Uhh... You can come on in, I guess..." The strong scent of her perfume clouds his judgement, and he gestures to a kitchen chair. "Have a seat."

"Will you please lock the door?"

Clive glances to the assortment of locks on the old, paint-crusted door and locks only one of them. He turns back and looks her over curiously. "What is this all about?"

"I need your help."

"You already mentioned that."

"Are you on the case of the Santa Monica Sniper?"

Taken aback, the private investigator doesn't hide his surprise. When she doesn't inquire further, he finally responds, "How do you mean?"

"I saw you on the news today."

"You did? Why would I be of interest?"

"They did a big feature story about you, and how you caught that famous kidnapper for the police in eighty-five."

"Those are pretty old headlines."

"It was the biggest high-profile kidnapping case since the Lindbergh baby."

"That may be, but it also happened a long time ago. Where did you get the idea that I'm on the sniper case?"

"You're all over the news."

"How old is your television set?"

She doesn't understand his witty joke and continues. "Every news channel out there has picked up the story."

"What story are you talking about?"

"That you're the special investigator brought in on the case of the Santa Monica Sniper…"

"The special investigator? What… They *did*?"

Catherine stops to catch her breath and takes on a look of concern. "You *are* on the case, Mr. Wilts, aren't you?"

Thinking quickly, he puffs his chest and responds confidently. "How did you find me?"

"You're in the phone book."

"Oh, yeah… Right. So, what do you need my help with? As you can guess, I'm very busy at the moment."

Catherine takes a deep breath, looks past him into the living room area and whispers, "Are we alone?"

Clive almost breaks out laughing but retains his stoic posture. "Uh, yes… I currently do not have any other guests."

"I need you to find out the identity of the shooter for me. It's imperative that I know who it is before the police do."

Clive furrows his brow and studies the woman seated at his kitchen table. "Do you think it's a friend or relative?"

"No."

"Okay, I'll bite. Why?"

"I have personal reasons… You'll be paid well."

Suspicious, Clive smooths his hand over his thin hair and shakes his head. "Personal reasons don't impress me much. First off, if I was to work for you, I would need to know where your interests lie. Why don't you come by my office tomorrow, and we'll talk about it." Reaching over toward the refrigerator, Clive grabs a business card from the stack on top and offers it to her at a distance, baiting her to stand and accept it.

Staying seated, she pleads, "Can't we talk about it *now*?"

Clive holds the business card outstretched and inches it to her a bit more. "No, tomorrow is better. In the daylight, things become much clearer."

Finally, she stands up and takes the card. As she reads the office address, Clive slips around behind her and ushers her toward the door. She looks back at him. "What time?"

He quickly unlocks the door and scoots her outside. "Whenever it's convenient for you. Good night now..."

Catherine looks at the business card again and sighs. "Alright... Tomorrow, then... Please don't accept any other cases about it until we meet."

Humoring her, Clive nods his head. "Fine. I will turn down all offers until tomorrow." Clive pops his head out and peers curiously down both directions of the empty hallway. Satisfied that this isn't some joke, he smiles at her courteously and then shuts the door.

Leaving Catherine alone in the hall, Clive fastens the three locks on the door and walks away to the kitchen. Then, quietly, he creeps back to the door and peeks out the peephole. He looks out to see that Catherine is still standing there with his business card in her hand. Pensive, she taps the card on her open palm a few times and then walks away.

Chapter 8

The chatter from the crowd behind the neighborhood bar increases as the night progresses. Carrying his unfinished beer, Clive returns to the other room and sits on the couch again. Awake now, he grabs the remote control from atop a pile of magazines on the coffee table, clicks the television set on and flips through the news channels.

Suddenly, a familiar headshot of him pops on the screen, swipes to the upper corner, followed by recent footage of him leaving the Santa Monica Police Station. Clive glances to an old newspaper clipping on the wall. It displays the same profile picture under the front-page headline. He looks back to the newscast to see a playback from today of him getting into his car and pulling out from the parking spot between the two squad cars. A gasp escapes his lips. "Ahh, shit..."

The news footage ends with the red Fiero pulling into the street with a screech of tires, and another car honking as it swerves from its own lane of travel. The next video has a television reporter standing in front of the police station, while multiple news crews set up in the background. Clive feels his face flush and his stomach turn as he hears the newscast:

"I'm at the Santa Monica Police Station where, earlier today, the renowned private investigator, Clive Wilts, known from the nineteen eighty-five kidnapping case of 'Billionaire Baby Barrow', was seen leaving. As we all have come to know, he was the deciding factor that turned the difficult case around for the detectives, and now

it seems that the police department has yet again called on his services to untangle this current spree of murder."

The newscast splits the screen with clear footage from a helicopter camera. The bird's eye view shows Clive's car pulling up and parking in a red zone near the location of the first shooting. The reporter continues:

"Although informed by key officials within the Santa Monica Police Department that any connection of Mr. Wilts with the case is unfounded, it is obvious from footage taken earlier today at the scene of the very first murder, that Detective Clive Wilts' collaboration with local law enforcement will again be an important factor in the apprehension of the Santa Monica Sniper."

The aerial video ends with the little red sports car driving away, as the Meter Maid patrol cart approaches along the line of parked cars. Wrapping up the news segment, the handsome reporter smiles into the camera lens and states:

"Hopefully, he will bring a speedy end to these assassinations of public servants. Back to you at the studio, Phil..."

Clive clicks the television set off and lays his head back. He takes a deep breath and groans, "This is bad... Real bad." The phone beside him rings, and he reaches over to pick it up. He listens a moment, swallows and replies, "Yes, I just saw it... I don't know where they got that story... Uh, yeah, I guess so. There should be a young woman that comes in tomorrow about the case... Gosh, I don't know. Try to pump some information out of her. Okay, yeah... See ya tomorrow." He hangs up the phone and wipes a hand over his sweat-dampened forehead. "There goes the rest of my reputation..."

~*~

Clive drives up in front of the neighborhood coffee shop and slides into a parking spot surprisingly close to the entrance. He hops out and looks cautiously down the street, both ways. "No journalists or news cameras around... That's a good start."

On the way to the door, he glances back down the sidewalk to double check and then goes inside.

At the counter, Clive orders his regular coffee and Danish, and then he finds an empty seat to wait for someone to finish their paper. He pulls out his cell phone, flips it open and goes through the same routine of trying to get a signal. Suddenly, the phone rings and, surprised, he nearly drops it.

He looks to the caller identification on the display, nervously puts the phone to his ear and speaks. "Uh, hello?" Clive looks around at the other occupants in the coffee shop, but no one seems to notice him. The barking voice on the other end of the call is highly irritated. Clive responds with, "Hold it. Not fair, I had nothing to do with it! Yes, I did see the news. No… No, that was*n't* my idea of a funny joke."

He looks around the coffee shop again and sheepishly covers his hand over the earpiece of the phone, so no one can hear the elevated tone of the irate caller. Putting the phone just close enough to his ear to hear, he replies, "You want me to come down to the station? Okay, okay… Lunch would be fine. But, not in Santa Monica…?" Clive looks around the coffee shop again. Seeing that no one really cares about his phone call, he gingerly moves the receiver closer to his ear as the voice on the other end of the line finally takes a breath and settles down. "How about Roscoe's…? Alright, see you there at noon. Bye…"

As Clive is about to hang up, his daily infatuation walks in and gives him her usual friendly smile. He looks at his phone to see that the call has disconnected and boldly speaks again. "Yeah… Sure, Buckley… I'll be there. No, I won't be followed. Just trust me. *Ciao!*" Clive flips the cell phone closed before she can see the blank display, and looks up as she stops at his table. He slips his phone into the pocket of his sport coat and utters, "Oh, Hello, there… Good morning."

She smiles and shifts a newspaper folded underneath her arm. "Good morning, Magnum…" She drops the daily paper to the table, spreads it open and flips to the second page. "Or, should I say… *The Hero Detective of Southern California - Clive Wilts*?" Clive's jaw nearly drops, as he sees the photo of him from years ago and a full-page write-up about him being attached to the Santa Monica Sniper case. She gazes at him, impressed, and asks, "May I have a seat?"

Clive pulls the newspaper closer and quickly scans the details of the story. "Uh, yeah… Sure… Please…"

The young woman slides into the chair across from Clive and smiles sweetly. "I see you almost every morning here, but we've never been properly introduced."

As he skims over the article, he develops a nervous trickle of sweat on his brow. Distracted, he looks up at her and replies. "Huh…?"

Smiling, she reaches her hand out across the table to shake his. "Hello. My name is Maryanne."

For a moment, Clive stares blankly at her before snapping out of it. "Yes, I know."

Surprised at his reaction, she takes her hand back and replies, "Of course you would, being a detective and all."

Clive folds the newspaper over and composes himself. "What I mean is, I read your name on your coffee order once. We were standing at the pay counter together about a year ago, back when you first called me Magnum."

Maryanne suddenly becomes embarrassed and fiddles with the top of the purse on her lap. "I'm so sorry about that. The flashy Hawaiian shirts were too much for me to pass up." She looks away and back again. "I thought I was being cute, and you just kept being so nice about it."

Clive takes a sip of his coffee, shrugs and stuffs the rest of his breakfast Danish into his mouth. "Actually, I don't mind, and it makes my day to hear it."

She self-consciously flushes again and looks to the coffee counter. "I'm going to get something... Do you want anything? I would love to treat you, of course."

He looks at his wristwatch, feels for his phone in his jacket pocket and winces. "Actually, I have to run."

"Oh, yeah... Big case..."

Clive pauses briefly before giving her a big smile accompanied by a broad wink. "You bet." After another glance at the newspaper, he takes the last gulp of his coffee.

Maryanne scoots the paper to him. "Do you want this?"

"What?"

"The newspaper..."

"Uh, sure..."

"I noticed that you usually read a paper every morning, and I got this one just for you."

"You did?"

She smiles, as she glances over at a person getting up from the next table and leaving their newspaper unattended. "And, you don't have to wait for it."

A bit embarrassed, Clive folds the paper over and tucks it under his arm. "Thanks, Maryanne."

"See ya later, Magnum."

With renewed pep in his step, Clive heads to the door and turns around to wave at her. "See ya later, Shweetheart." Pushing past the door, he trots across the sidewalk and does a leap into his Fiero through the open window and T-top roof. He starts the car, revs the engine a few times, cranks the steering wheel to pull out of his prime parking spot, and then zooms down the street.

Chapter 9

Lining the street in front of his North Hollywood office building, Clive notices several news vans set up and a gathering crowd. He drives by, murmuring to himself, "Where's the accident?" Turning into the parking lot adjacent to his building, Clive pulls into his regular spot, shifts the car to park, and shuts off the engine.

Before Clive can exit the vehicle, he is approached by several television reporters, each followed by a camera crew. One of the news reporters leans his face down to the driver's side window and shouts through the glass. "Detective Wilts, what kind of leads do you have?"

Another reporter nudges in and holds a microphone against the window, questioning, "How soon until you catch the shooter? Is it a him or a her?"

Clive grabs his newspaper from the passenger seat, and pushes into the correspondents when he opens the car door. The other news teams scurry around the front corner of the building to cluster around Clive. Raising his hands, he waits for quiet and then announces, "Guys, I am not at liberty to make a statement at this time." Clive squeezes through a flurry of questions and prodding microphones, as he makes his way past the crowd of reporters to the front of the office building. Blocking the entry, the Meter Maid from the previous day stands waiting. Clive sees her and murmurs, "Oh, shit..."

Clive looks around as he approaches the parking enforcement officer, grateful for the protection of the news cameras pointed at him. Cautiously, he nods a hello and, surprisingly, the Meter Maid smiles, offering her praises. "Detective. Wilts, I want to apologize to you for yesterday. You're a wonderful man!" The cameras and microphones oscillate from Clive to the Meter Maid and then back again.

Nodding with humble acceptance, Clive stammers, "Yeah, uh, no problem..."

As she continues, the reporters turn their microphones to the Meter Maid again. "I just know you'll get the shooter. We're all rooting for you. Bless you, Mr. Wilts!"

Ducking into the front entrance of the building, Clive runs up the stairway followed closely by the camera crews. When he gets to his office, he turns the doorknob and bumps into a locked door. With the crowd of reporters coming up from behind, he hollers desperately through the frosted glass window. "Delores! *Open the door!* It's me! *Clive...!*"

The inside lock clicks, and the door cracks partly open. Delores peeks out and utters, "Mr. Wilts? Is that you?" Immediately recognizing her boss, she swings the door open. Clive tumbles inside, before the door is slammed back shut and locked behind him.

In a troubled daze, Clive gets up from the office floor, dusts himself off and looks around the empty reception area. Delores stands braced against the locked door. The window, with the shadows of the multiple chattering people outside, rattles behind her. She looks at him and states, "They got here this morning and have been very persistent."

He smooths a hand over his head to fix his hair and takes a deep breath. "Not only am I not officially on the sniper case, but I can't even get near it with all these *civets* around."

Delores looks at him curiously. "*Civet...?* What's that?"

Citation for Murder

"I heard it spouted the other day from Mr. Goldleffer. Look it up for me, please. I'm not sure, but I think it's bad."

The receptionist rechecks the lock on the door and then steps away from the entry. "If you heard it from that crusty fart, it probably isn't a very nice thing." She goes to her desk, grabs a note pad, writes down *civet*, and then reads his messages, "That gal you mentioned on the phone last night called in."

After peeking over at the other scribbles on her notepad, Clive walks to his office, opens the door and wonders aloud, "Yeah? Is she actually going to come by?"

Delores follows into his office, as Clive goes to his desk. She flips on the overhead light, and the florescent bulbs flicker. At the bay of windows, Clive looks down at the news crews lined up on the street. Reading from her notes, Delores reports, "Said she couldn't be seen by all the press outside and wants to meet with you later this afternoon. Somewhere private…"

Clive pulls up the blinds and cranks open a window. While he counts the number of news vans, someone spots him from the street and, as if on cue, the cameras all turn upward. Clive ducks back inside and quickly closes the window. "Jeez…!" Taking a seat in his chair, he faces his desktop and then plops his face down on the stack of folders before him.

With her notepad and pen at the ready, Delores steps closer to the desk and leans down to see if her boss is okay. "Mister Wilts… What do you want to do?"

"Ahhh… They'll go away eventually."

She goes over and has a peek at the media circus outside the windows. "What about the meeting with that woman?"

"Who?"

"The woman who visited you last night."

"What's her name?"

"Catherine."

Sitting up and pushing back in his chair, Clive puts his hands on top of his head and looks at Delores across the desk. "There was something very familiar about her. Did she say where she wants to meet?"

"Griffith Observatory at one o'clock…"

"I thought she wanted someplace private?"

"She said to take a walk around to the back."

He thinks a moment and then nods. "That will be fine. Give her a return call to confirm." As Delores turns and makes her way to the doorway, Clive squints at the overhead lights. "Shut off those lights."

She nods and flips off the switch on her way out. "Anything else, Mr. Wilts?"

"Be sure to look up civet, will ya?" She rolls her eyes and begins to close the door behind her, when Clive shouts, "And, I need to meet with Buckley at Roscoe's for lunch today at noon. If those jackals are still out there, I'm going to need you to pull my car around from the parking lot and leave it down the block around eleven o'clock."

"Mind if I run some of them over on my way?"

Clive slides a desk drawer open and searches through the cluttered contents. "Sure… Just don't hit any of those guys with cameras. I heard it directly from Jack Nicholson that they're very expensive."

Smiling, the receptionist flips her notepad shut and pulls the door closed. "Yes, Mister Wilts…"

Chapter 10

A canvas duffle bag sits open on Clive's desk. He goes over to peek out the window again, then quickly ducks back. "Wow, it's insane out there!" The detective looks over the items placed on his desk and counts the multiple rolls of film canisters lined up next to the bag. Satisfied with the number, he scoops them all up and dumps them, along with his camera, into the bag. There is a soft tap on Clive's office door and Delores pops her head in. He zips his bag and looks at her. "Are we all set to go?"

"Whenever you're ready, Mr. Wilts."

Grabbing the duffle by the handles, Clive moves around the desk and follows Delores out into the main office. They go to the front entry, put an ear to the door, and listen for any news reporters outside. He looks to her and shrugs. "Okay...?"

"I'm not sure, Mr. Wilts."

"Let's take a look and see. If the hall is clear, I'm going to head for the men's bathroom and sneak down the fire escape. Take my car around to the laundromat and wait for me."

"Sure thing, Mr. Wilts..."

"If they follow you, or if you have any sort of problem, give me a call on my cell phone."

"Anything else...?"

"Well, depending on how things play out with Buckley, I might not be back to the office this afternoon."

"Do I need to come up with bail money?"

Clive gives her a scolding look and shakes his head. "Buckley said he wanted to meet with me, not arrest me." Delores shrugs, as Clive adds, "I think…"

After unlocking the door, Delores peeks outside before opening it a bit further and stepping into the hallway. She looks back at Clive, nods, and gives a wave. "Looks to be all clear."

"Alright… See you in a bit…" Clive slips past her and shuffles quietly down the hall toward the public bathrooms. She watches him go into the men's room, and she then gets the keys from her purse to lock the office door. The sound of a window slamming open grabs her attention, and she looks down the hallway to the bathrooms again. She locks the office, tucks her purse under her arm and walks away while hearing the creaking of the fire escape stairway. She looks back briefly, listens to the rattle of the rusty metal hinges, and then makes her way down the stairs to the front of the building.

~*~

Delores exits the office building and is instantly surrounded by multiple news cameras and eager reporters. With probing microphones on all sides, she works her way through the crowd, down the sidewalk, and around the corner toward Clive's car in the parking lot. After making it to the sports car, she takes a key from her coat pocket, unlocks the door and ducks inside. As microphones thump at every window, she waves them away, then starts the engine and puts the car in reverse. Backing out of the parking spot, nudging through the crowd, she turns the steering wheel to point the car out to the street. Pulling forward, she rolls down her window a tiny bit and tells the eager reporters, "Mr. Wilts is unavailable and says *No Comment*."

~*~

Clive steps off from the bottom tread of the fire-escape stairway and reaches out to catch it as the stairs start to rise.

Missing, and the metal stairway lifts swiftly upward and resets with a loud, rattling *bang*. Chagrined, Clive hunches his shoulders, and looks down the empty alleyway. When no one appears to have noticed the noise, he hurries around the corner toward the laundromat.

~*~

Waiting out front of the Soap 'N Suds Laundromat, Clive peers over at a newspaper vending machine and scans the headlines about the recent shootings. Hearing his car arrive, he turns to see Delores pull into the lot. She shuts off the engine, shimmies out of the low-profile car and adjusts her snug, knee-length skirt. Clive grabs his duffle from the bench and meets her at the car door. "You have any problems?"

She takes a calming breath and hands over the car key. "Those reporters are *definitely* of the civet species."

"You looked it up?"

"Yes, and it's not flattering."

Clive slips behind the wheel. "Gotta go! Tell me later..." She shuts his door and peers down through the dark-tinted roof, as Clive starts the car, pops it in reverse and backs away. She watches him pull into the street and doesn't notice that he is shadowed by an older model, primer-grey Honda Civic.

~*~

Clive stands outside of Roscoe's Chicken & Waffles. Waiting, he glances at his wristwatch, looks down the street, and then takes off his aviator sunglasses to clean them with the front of his shirt. He puts his sunshades back on and casually notices an older Honda Civic, in need of a paint job, making its third pass around the block before pulling into a parking spot just down the street.

From the other direction, Detective Buckley steps out of an unmarked police car and approaches. As he walks nearer, he calls out. "Hey Clive! You eat already?"

The private investigator turns to the police detective and then glances back up the street to the primer-grey car. Shrugging-off the repeated sighting of the Honda as mere coincidence, he replies, "Not yet… Waiting on you."

Chapter 11

The two men take seats on opposite sides of the table with their chicken and waffle dinners. The police detective looks at the tray of hot food and, before he starts to eat, addresses Clive. "You got us into a fine mess." As the private investigator looks at him, doesn't reply and starts to eat, Buckley continues. "How'd you get your face all over the press so quickly?"

Clive chews his food and swallows before answering. "Figured *your* guys did it…"

Buckley stirs some gravy into his mashed potatoes. "Why would you think that?"

"Decoy…"

"We don't use decoys."

Clive finishes a chicken wing and starts in on another. He licks his fingertips and turns his gaze toward Buckley. "Yeah, sure…"

As Clive eats, Buckley watches, takes a bite of his own food and then wipes his mouth. "Would you be interested?"

Clive stares over his plate at Buckley and shakes his head. "I'm not dressing up in a Halloween costume and posing as a Meter Maid, if that's what you're thinking."

Buckley lowers his voice. "No, no… Nothing like that… We just need someone to keep the cameras off us, so we can do our job and catch this guy."

"What did you have in mind?"

Warily, the police detective looks around the restaurant to make sure no one is listening. He leans forward on the table. "Well, we could unofficially bring you in on the investigation. We'll have you shadow a Parking Enforcement Officer... Then, we could observe a possible target without being watched."

Clive nibbles at a chicken wing, pulls it apart, and picks at the small bones. "Why? Do you think he'll bite?"

"There's been so much over-hyped news coverage about you being the super sleuth of the ages, that I don't think he'll be able to resist." Buckley starts to eat. "Seeing your face all over the news makes *me* want to take a shot at you."

"Thanks..."

Buckley uses his napkin to wipe the grin from his face.

Stacking his chicken bones at the edge of his plate, Clive stops chewing and thinks a minute. He dabs his mouth with a napkin and then picks up another wing piece. "It reeks of a trap. No one would go for it."

The detective mulls over his meal, talking as he chews. "Come on, Wilts... The people who do this sort of stuff aren't the brightest. Ninety-five percent of the time, they're morons who just want to get their name in the paper and a shot on TV." Buckley inspects an odd shaped piece of chicken, puts it down and stares at Clive. "The deal is this... You follow the target, and the news crews follow you. He won't be able to resist the attention, and then we'll come in and grab him."

"You keep referring to him as a *he*..."

"*He, she, it*... Whatever!"

Clive thinks as he chews a mouthful of food, and then he takes another. He considers the proposed scenario and then, while his mouth is still full, he responds. "You guys gonna give me a *real* Meter Maid to follow?"

Buckley nods, looking serious. "Yeah, have to. None of our people will volunteer to do it. They'll go without showers and sleep in a city gutter for a month to catch a drug dealer, but they won't demean themselves to play a Meter Maid for a day."

After wiping his chin with a napkin, Clive pushes his plate away. "How about the pay?"

"What did you have in mind?"

"My regular rate, along with a hazard bonus..."

Buckley grimaces. "What hazard? He'll be aiming at the Meter Maid."

"What if he misses?"

"He hasn't yet."

"*You* do it, then."

"Fine! Hazard pay, too."

"When do I start?"

Buckley pulls out a folded piece of paper and slides it over to Clive. "Here's the contact info for the meter-jockey. Give the number a call and set up a time to meet."

Clive takes the folded paper and taps it on the table. "Does the Meter Maid know about this great plan of yours?"

"Sort of..."

"Is she expecting me?"

"I think it's a he, and he is."

Clive nods and, without taking a peek at the folded note, tucks it away in his coat pocket. "Okay. I'll do it."

"Good... I figured you would."

"I have another appointment, and then I'll be on it."

The detective starts in on his lunch again and nods. "Fine. All you have to do is hang around the scene to lure the shooter out. And remember... *We're* the ones who'll nab him."

Clive lets out a giggle. "Not like last time...?"

Mid-swallow, Buckley sternly looks across the table at him. "Clive, I mean it... No showboating on this one."

"I can't guarantee anything, or what gets in the papers. Sometimes I'm just in the right place..."

Coughing his throat clear, Buckley interrupts, "When the bullets fly, be sure you're not in the *wrong* place."

"Or, on the wrong boat…"

The detective swallows and nearly chokes, as he gives Clive a chastising look. "Do you *always* have to be an ass?"

Pleased with himself, Clive gets up from the table and looks out the front window. He spots the primer-grey Honda Civic still parked down the street and can make out the form of someone still sitting inside. He turns to Buckley and questions, "Do your boys drive Honda Civics now?"

"No… Why?"

"I think I may have my *own* shadow…"

Chewing on another bite, Buckley leans over the table to peer out the window. He rolls his eyes sarcastically and utters, "Want me to shoot his tires out?"

"I can handle it." Heading for the door, Clive turns back and shakes a finger at Buckley who is still finishing his meal. "You know where to send the check!" The police detective nods and scoops up another forkful of mashed potatoes.

Clive steps outside the restaurant, puts on his shades, and then looks at his wristwatch: 12:45 pm. He scans the line of cars along the street, makes a mental note of the parked Honda, and then walks to his vehicle. He slides into his car, starts it up, revs the engine and peels out into the flow of traffic. Clive looks to his rearview mirror, and notices that the grey-primed vehicle pulls out a few car-lengths behind him.

Chapter 12

The little red sports car zooms up a winding, two-lane road toward the Griffith Park Observatory. Clive occasionally checks his rearview mirror and sees that the Honda Civic, at a good distance, still tails him. He down-shifts into a lower gear, revs the engine and, heading uphill, zips around a hairpin turn. "Let's see how good you are..."

Momentarily out of the sight of the car following him, Clive scans a winding line of parked vehicles pulled to the dirt shoulder and sees an open spot at the hiking trailhead. He quickly slips the Fiero into the space, slams the car into *park*, takes his foot off the brake pedal and leaves the engine running. Crouching down in the seat, he watches the Honda from the side-view mirror as it approaches and drives on by.

Getting a clear view of the driver, who appears to be alone in the vehicle, Clive grimaces. "Hmm... Do I know you?" After a short wait, Clive straightens up in his seat, adjusts his coat and looks at the clock on the car radio. Shifting into gear, he pulls out and, revving the engine, continues driving up the steep hill toward the observatory.

~*~

Arriving at the parking area in front of the building, Clive searches for a space and finally finds one between two large SUVs. He hops out and walks toward the main entry. Waiting a few minutes, he checks the time on his wristwatch: 1:00 pm exactly. He looks back toward the parking lot. Then, when he follows the sidewalk that circles to the back of the observatory, he hears his name called from behind a large, blooming yucca plant. He looks down the hillside at the edge of the walkway and hears it again.

"Clive Wilts...!"

"Hello?"

"Are you alone?"

"I came here by myself." Clive looks over his shoulder to see that he wasn't tailed, realizing how ridiculous talking to a plant looks.

"Were you followed?"

"It's just me."

"Are you sure?"

Beginning to feel impatient, Clive looks again to the observatory parking lot and sees that no one is following. "Catherine, come on out here and talk to me, or I'm leaving." Clive waits a moment until, smiling sheepishly, she finally comes out from behind the yucca. He looks at her suspiciously. "What are you doing back there?"

"I didn't want anyone to recognize or follow me."

"Why would anyone follow you?"

She looks around carefully to verify that they are alone. "If you haven't noticed already, this town is full of cameras. Seeing what it was like in front of your office today, I didn't want to be in someone else's footage for the evening news."

Clive looks to the front entrance of the popular tourist destination, where almost everyone has a camera around their neck or a camcorder in hand. He shrugs, dismissing them as sightseers. "That's no reason to hide yourself behind a plant."

Suddenly embarrassed, Catherine gets a bit defensive. "Oh, really? You, being a private investigator, have never had to hide in whatever vegetation is available?"

Clive blushes and changes the subject. "What did you want to meet me about?"

Still self-conscious, she looks around again to confirm that they are alone. "I told you last night that I needed your help to identify the Santa Monica Sniper." She lowers her voice to a soft whisper. "I need to identify this person before the police do. It's very important that I do this."

Clive is skeptical of her extremely cautious behavior. "What makes it so important? Revenge?"

"I can't tell you. It's a personal matter..."

He shakes his head, unconvinced. "I told you before, that's not enough to go on. I need to know how I'm going to keep my butt out of the hoosegow."

The woman steps closer and leans into him, pleading. "*Please*, Mister Wilts...I really *need* this. It is very important that I get pictures of the sniper *before* he is caught."

"He?"

"Or she... Whomever!"

"You need pictures?"

"Yes, I need a photograph before they catch the shooter, so I can verify the identity."

Not believing what he's hearing, Clive takes a step back. "Are you off your nut, lady?"

She matches his retreating step, presents an overstuffed white envelope, and in a whisper says, "There's five hundred dollars in here."

He looks down at the thick wad and crinkles his brow. "It looks like more than that." She glimpses around to be sure that they are still alone and replies guiltily. "I had to get it in twenties from the ATM." Suggestively, she slides the envelope full of cash into his inside coat pocket and continues in her low, breathy voice. "Another five hundred when you get me photos, and double that, if you let me know when you catch him."

With contempt, he peers down at her hand, which is still on his chest. "Do you realize that if I were to get a positive photo of the sniper, he would have to have his cross-hairs on some poor sap of a Meter Maid?"

"So? One more couldn't hurt…"

Clive looks her in the eye and pushes her hand away. "Jeez, lady… They're lonely, pitiful, miserable outcasts as it is. They don't need someone shooting at them, too! Gosh…"

Catherine notices that, though he remains reluctant, he hasn't removed the money from his pocket. Shifting her tactics, she attempts to look uncaring and smiles. "Tell you what… Keep the money and think on it. While you're on the case, should the opportunity come up, all you have to do is simply snap a photo. Just let me know *first*…"

Unconvinced, he studies her with a sidelong glance. "You look familiar. Do I know you from somewhere?"

Catherine turns her face away. "This is Los Angeles… Everyone looks familiar." She scans the crowd of tourists in front of the observatory and turns back to him. "Think about it, My contact number is in the envelope. I'll be in touch."

Clive impulsively touches his hand to the wad of money in his sport coat pocket. "I'm not going to let anyone die to get you those pictures."

"I'm not asking you to…"

"Okay… Fine."

"Great."

Satisfied with his negotiating skills, Clive gives a nod. "I'll let you know if anything turns up."

"Fair enough… Remember, Mr. Wilts, call me first, before anyone else."

Clive watches her descend the hillside and creep back into the vegetation. After she disappears behind the blooming yucca, he can hear her sliding down in the dirt. Rolling his eyes, he comments, "I'm usually the one who has to retreat through the bushes…" He protectively pats the envelope of cash in his pocket and walks back toward the observatory parking lot.

Chapter 13

While approaching his Fiero, Clive spots the young man who was following him, lurking around and peeking in his car. Stealthily moving toward him, the private investigator drops his gaze to the pavement, so as not to alert him to his presence. From just a few feet away, the guy turns, recognizes Clive and tries to make a run for it. Lunging forward, Clive pins him face-first to the side of the larger SUV parked alongside his car. "Hold on there, mister!"

"Hey! Let me go! I didn't do anything…"

Clive peels the guy from the rear panel of the vehicle and spins him around to get a good look at his face. He presses him, "What's your name, kid?"

The young man doesn't answer and, instead, looks around, ready to call for help from anyone who might pass by. As the kid backpedals, Clive releases his hold and grumbles, "Tough guy, huh…? You're not gonna tell me anything, eh?" The kid suddenly freezes when he sees Clive flip open a wallet and then begin to read: "Francis W. Johnston. Five-foot-five, one hundred and sixty pounds. Says here, he lives at twenty-two-thirteen Crescent Hills Drive, Sherman Oaks."

Stunned, the kid stares then utters, "Where did you get that?" He steps toward Clive and makes a grab for the wallet. "Give me that! How did you get that?"

Clive holds out the wallet, teasingly dangling it in front of Francis. "You must have dropped it."

"Give it back to me!"

"How do I know it's yours?"

Francis stops in his tracks and takes a breath of defeat. "It's mine. Just give it back."

Staying an arm's reach away while keeping an eye on Francis, Clive thumbs through the numerous credit cards and few small bills of cash. "You aren't rich. And, for a Boy Scout, you should have better manners than to be following people." He flips the wallet closed and tosses it. "If I was to guess... With that number of credit cards, I'd say you were an actor." Astonished, the young man slides his wallet into his hip pocket and looks at the investigator. When Clive doesn't get a confirming answer, he asks, "Am I correct?"

"Yeah... So?"

"What are you doing following me?"

Francis takes a small step back, as if he's ready to bolt. Casually, Clive leans on the side of his car and plays with a set of keys. He looks at the big one on the ring which reads: *Honda*. He adds, coolly, "You might as well answer my questions. You're not going far without your car keys."

Completely taken aback, the kid stops. He mutters, "Jeez, mister... Did you clean out *all* my pockets?"

"All except the one with the Kleenex..." Francis pats his pockets silently. Clive waits for answers, doesn't receive any, and queries once again. "Why are you following me, Francis?"

"I'm researching a role."

This time, Clive is the one who is taken by surprise. "What kind of a role?"

"You."

"Me?"

Obviously relieved to finally reveal his secret and be face-to-face with his character-model, Francis lets it all spill out.

"The studio bought the rights to the *Santa Monica Sniper* story, and I'm soliciting to get the part playing you."

"What do you mean, *bought the rights*? From *who*?"

Francis smiles and shrugs innocently. "I don't know. They just announced in the trade papers that they bought the film rights, and they have writers working on it now."

"How will that work?

"I don't know… That's not my job."

"Is there a *happily ever after*?"

The young man doesn't get the humor, but he excitedly adds, "They are doing some preliminary casting, and I am in the running for your part."

Taking a step back, looking for a candid-camera crew, Clive looks down the aisle of cars and peeks around behind the SUV. "Is this a joke?"

Tilting his head, Francis looks at Clive like *he's* the one who is out of touch with reality. "It's a primo role!"

"You want to play *me*?"

"Yeah… So far…"

"And, you say they have writers working on it *now*?"

"Yep… Should be ready to film in a few weeks."

"How does it end?"

Francis shrugs as if the question is entirely irrelevant. "Doesn't matter… They'll spice it up."

Clive rolls his eyes and drops the look of disgust from his face. He tosses Francis the filched set of keys. "Get out of here, kid, and I better not see you following me around again." He thinks a second and adds, "If I do, you're not doing your job well, and I'll be sure to notify the first casting director I see."

Clive telling Francis that he is a hack actor, without the skills to research a role properly hits him hard, and he puts on a hang-dog expression. "Uh… Okay…"

Eric H. Heisner

"Trust me. If I sense you anywhere on my radar, you'll never work in this town again." Clive digs his own keys from his pocket and gets into his car. After starting it, he pokes his head up through the open roof and examines the young man from head to toe. "Oh, and Francis… If you want the important role of playing me in a movie, you need to be a much better dresser than that."

Francis looks down at his Salvation Army wardrobe of khaki pants, old boat shoes and Hawaiian shirt combination. He frowns with uncertainty. "Are you kidding?"

Clive drops back down into the driver's seat, backs the car out of the parking spot and shifts into gear. In warning, he wags a finger at Francis and then pulls away.

~*~

Zipping through traffic on Hollywood Boulevard, Clive gets caught at a stop light. While waiting for it to change green, he takes out the thick envelope from Catherine, opens it and thumbs through the stack of twenty-dollar bills. He gives a satisfied whistle, takes out a few, folds them and tucks them away in his pants pocket.

Recalling the note from Buckley, he takes out the folded paper, fumbles it open, and reads the name and phone number. Clive stares curiously at it for a moment, flips it over to see a blank backside, and, as the light changes, hears the blast of several car horns behind him. Waving his hand out the roof, Clive steps on the gas pedal and zooms ahead. He looks at the note again and reads aloud, *"John Smith…* Unbelievable… Might as well be *John Doe's* phone number. Or, *Jim Rockford at 555-2368…"*

Chapter 14

Cruising the car-lined streets of Santa Monica once again, Clive takes out his phone and flips it open. Surprised that he actually has a signal, he taps in the phone number written on the note. There is a long, soundless delay, and then an electronic ring-tone pulses. After a moment, someone answers, and Clive talks while he drives. "Hello, John...? This is Clive Wilts, Private Investigator... Yeah, the one in the news. Today is fine. Where do we meet? Okay. Be there in a few minutes."

~*~

The little red Fiero pulls up alongside a three-wheeled parking enforcement vehicle. Clive rolls down his passenger-side window and yells to the attendant sitting inside the cart. "Hey John... Clive Wilts here... We just talked on the phone. Anywhere I can park my car and not get a ticket?"

The uniformed officer looks over at him and smirks. "Not in Santa Monica..." As Clive tilts his head, not sure if the reply was a joke or not, John motions for him to drive ahead. "Pull up to that meter, and I'll decommission it."

After pulling into the open parking spot, Clive watches as John walks up and opens the back of the lollipop-shaped meter head. Before he rolls up the passenger-side window, he asks John, "What are you doing?"

"Adjusting the clock..."

"You can do that?"

With a cunning smile, John bends to look at Clive. "Yeah… We can speed it up, too." Clive observes, wide-eyed, as John goes back to fiddling with the insides of the meter head. Satisfied, the Meter Maid slaps the back cover closed and locks it. "There… We're good to go for the rest of my shift."

Clive shifts his car into park, rolls up the windows and murmurs to himself. "Okay… I guess I'll ride with *you*."

~*~

The three-wheeled parking enforcement vehicle rolls along with the two men stuffed inside, shoulder to shoulder. Clive watches the parking attendant intently scan the row of cars for anything remotely unlawful. When the cart slows, almost to a stop, Clive studies the cars and then questions, "What, exactly, are you looking for?"

"Oh, the usual… Like, any vehicle that isn't tagged local. The street signage is made to confuse people. The folks who don't park in this neighborhood regular are the ones to ticket." John continues his informative lecture without completely stopping the motored cart or interrupting his keen stare. "Other than that, I look for expired tags, license stickers, parking too close to a red zone or too far away from the curb. Did you know that any more than fifteen inches into the street, and I can get 'em? There is usually something I can find on *any* out-of-state plate."

Unsettled, Clive takes in all the information. "So, John, did you piss off someone at the police academy? How did you end up with this job?"

Suddenly, the cart stops, and John turns to glare at Clive. "What do you mean, *end up*?"

Put on the spot, the private investigator starts to perspire as the Meter Maid frowns at him. Not sure what to say, Clive stammers, "Well, I mean most kids dream of being doctors, firemen, or garbage men. What got you interested in this?"

Sullen, John scrutinizes Clive for almost a full minute. Then, the parking enforcement officer finally lets the sides of his lips creep upward into the hint of a smile. Clive takes a breath and utters feebly. "No offense intended…"

John continues his intent stare. "You really want to know why I became a Parking Enforcement Officer?"

"Uh, yeah, if it's not too personal."

He replies simply, "Power."

"Power?"

"Yep, the same reason you became a private eye."

Clive shifts uneasily in his seat and shakes his head. "Uh, I didn't become a private investigator to get power."

"Sure you did."

"No, I didn't."

"Yes, you did."

Clive glances outside and then back to John again, who is getting intense. "I don't think so."

"Are you telling me that when you find out the dirt on someone, things that no one else knows about, you don't feel a distinct sense of power over them?"

Clive raises his eyebrows. He ponders the idea, and then replies. "That's not why I do it, but I guess in a certain light, you could look at it that way."

John shrugs. "Same reason that sniper is popping off random Meter Maids… Creating fear is a huge power trip."

Clive lets the cynical comments sink in and then mutters, "You call them Meter *Maids*?"

"Sometimes, but don't tell anyone."

With the men still sitting snugly against one another, the small cart starts to pull forward again. While rolling along, the driver suddenly hits the brakes and blurts out, "Yes!!! Got one!" John grabs his ticket book and hops out.

Clive watches the parking attendant circle around the car and leans outside. "What did this one do?"

"Forty-five-minute park zone... I saw him here earlier."

Clive glances at his watch to see they haven't been out but a few minutes. "How do you know it's over the time?"

Not looking up, John proceeds to write the ticket as he replies. "Usually takes me about half an hour to do the loop. Figured I talked with you about fifteen minutes, more or less."

Clive nods and asks, "How much is the ticket?"

"Forty bucks."

The steep penalty makes Clive wince. He looks to the street signage down the block which has three different parking restrictions listed on the pole. Between street cleaning, night-time restrictions, and the forty-five-minute zone, there is a lot to decipher. Clive looks around for anyone approaching the car. "You don't give them a few minutes leeway to make sure?"

Confused, John lowers the ticket book and looks at Clive. "Why? Sign says forty-five minutes..."

"What if you're wrong?"

"Let them fight it, then." The Meter Maid gives a snide chuckle and continues writing the ticket. "Good luck dealing with the traffic court, though." Aghast, Clive shakes his head and readies his camera. Figuring this might be a prime opportunity for the gunman, he scans all around for the sniper. He clicks-off a few shots of the parking attendant and turns the lens up to the distant rooftops.

Finished with writing the ticket, John tears it from his booklet and stands next to the car. He's waiting for something. Clive watches the attendant, as if the man was begging to be a target. Finally, Clive asks, "What are you doing now?"

"Waiting to see if anyone comes to the car."

Clive bobs his head while keeping his camera ready. "Wow, that's very nice of you."

John gives Clive a funny look. "What is…?"

"You waiting to see if anyone comes out and then tearing up the ticket…"

John stares at Clive as if he is insane. "What planet are you *from*, man?"

Clive lamely utters, "Planet Hollywood…?"

"No, I just like to hold onto the ticket and put it on the car just as the owner approaches. Now, *that's* power!"

Clive snaps a picture of John and quickly adjusts the long lens, as he ducks lower in the parking enforcement vehicle. "Are you wearing a bullet-proof vest?"

"Yes."

"Good… You might need it."

Chapter 15

The parking enforcement cart pulls up to Clive's red Fiero and idles quietly. Clive watches the arrow on the meter linger just above the expiration time, while John scans the street for any obvious parking violations. After tossing his ticket book to the dashboard, John taps the armored vest under his uniform and sighs with disappointment. "Well, no luck today then, huh?"

"I guess you could say that."

"You coming out again tomorrow?"

Clive nods. "Yeah, sure… If you're up for it."

"I ain't been shot… Why wouldn't I be?"

"Same shift tomorrow?"

"Yep."

"How about we meet here? Around two o'clock…?"

John grips his hands on the cart's steering wheel and pretends to drive fast and crazy. "Sounds good. I'll be dodging bullets on the street 'til two! See ya then!" Stepping out to the street, Clive waves as John slams his foot on the gas pedal. Instead of peeling out, the underpowered three-wheeled cart quietly eases forward at a steady pace.

While adjusting the camera lens, Clive snaps a few more shots as John rolls down the street and then turns the corner. He opens his car and tosses his camera to the passenger seat. "What a waste of my time…"

Seated behind the wheel, Clive leans forward about to turn the ignition key when he faintly hears screeching tires and the muffled crash of vehicles colliding. He thinks for a second, then starts the car, pulls out, and rips down the street.

Tires smoking, Clive's car skids around the corner, drifts across the empty intersection and races to the accident site. Ahead, at the end of the block, the Meter Maid cart, with one spinning wheel off the ground and the engine still quietly whining, is t-boned into a parked car. Several motorists are stopped near the wreck, but no one is stepping out to help.

At the scene of the accident, Clive swerves his car to the near side of the street, snatches up his camera and climbs out. Sliding over a car hood, Clive calls out, "John… Are you okay?" The staring bystanders remain sitting in their vehicles, and Clive hollers, "Hey! Someone call the police!" Clive reaches in, shuts off the ignition of the parking enforcement vehicle and brushes broken glass from John's lap. After snapping a photo of the bullet-shattered windshield, Clive holds a finger to John's neck and feels for a pulse. Successfully finding it, he hollers to the forming crowd, "He's alive. Call an ambulance!"

Someone gets on their phone to make the call, and Clive peers over the cart to scan the surrounding neighborhood. Instinctively, he flips the automatic shutter switch on his camera and snaps a continuous panoramic shot of the location. He does nearly two complete circles before the film runs out.

A gawking spectator steps forward to yell at Clive. "Hey, buddy… Who the hell said you could take my picture?"

Defiantly, Clive aims the camera at him and clicks it again. "Shoot… If you don't like it buddy, you'd better get out of here before the cops show up."

"How about I kick your ass?

"Really?"

"Yeah, and smash your camera!"

Seeing a black and white police cruiser turning the corner down the block, Clive gets a bit of false confidence.

"Better do it quick, tough guy, 'cause here they come now..." The loud blip of a siren turns heads in the crowd to the approaching vehicle, and most of the gawkers, including the hostile spectator, disperse.

Clive calmly addresses the remaining bystanders. "Anyone see what happened?" He is met by blank stares. Frustrated, he grimaces and pats his pockets in the hope of finding some of his business cards. Realizing they are in the pocket of the coat he left in his car, he announces to the ogling crowd. "If you don't want the hassle of talking to the police, you can phone me with any information you might remember. The name is *Clive Wilts, P I*, and I'm in the phone book."

Reaching into the cart to feel for the wounded man's pulse again, Clive pats John on the shoulder of his flack vest. "Hang in there... You're doing okay, and help is on the way."

A police officer comes up to them and accesses the situation. He calls to the crowd. "Anyone see what happened?" He is met with the same blank stares and total lack of response. Clive backs away from the crash and reports to the policeman. "He has a gunshot wound to the upper chest and right forearm. He's got a vest on, but you'd better get a meat-wagon here."

The police officer looks at Clive and then peers at the wounded parking attendant inside the cart. He motions for the lingering bystanders to move away. "Everyone, move back!" He looks at Clive. "Stick around, buddy."

The radio receiver on the officer's chest squawks with urgent chatter, and Clive looks around to see more police cars swarming to the scene. Overhearing that an ambulance is on the way, he backpedals into the circle of onlookers. The officer does his best to manage the site, keeping the encroaching crowd at bay so emergency personnel can gain access.

Not seeing how he can be of any help, Clive calls out to the policeman. "Hello, Officer..." When the policeman turns,

Clive tells him, "Have Detective Buckley give me a call if there are any questions."

"Who are you?"

"Clive Wilts…"

In the midst of the mounting confusion, the officer points a finger at Clive and yells, "Stick around!"

With a feeble shrug, Clive waits another few minutes. He watches as the ambulance arrives, and the medical team rushes to the scene. John is pulled from the crashed vehicle, placed on a stretcher and carried away. Playing to the crowd, the Meter Maid sits up and pumps his bloody fist in the air. When Clive sees several news crews approaching, he slowly backs up even more and then discreetly disappears into the crowd of gawkers.

~*~

In the early evening, with some light still in the sky, Clive cruises past his office building and sees that several news teams are still lingering out front. Circling the block once more, he makes note of the television channel logos on the side of the crew vans and continues to drive on. He clicks on his car radio to find a newscast. After listening to several unexciting topics, Clive switches to eighties music and presses on the gas pedal.

~*~

After finally finding a parking spot at the end of his street, Clive walks to his apartment building. He enters the hallway, and quickly ducks to the side when he sees people hanging out by his front door. "Now, who the heck are *they*?" He quietly slips back outside, walks around to the side of the building and heads toward the rear entrance.

In the back alley a news van is parked with the transmission antenna fully extended skyward. Nonchalantly, Clive walks up alongside the van and peeks inside the open driver-side window. He spots a set of keys in the center console.

Clive looks over his shoulder to be sure that no one is around, hesitates, and then murmurs, "Hate to do this..."

Reaching through the van's window, Clive slides the keys into the ignition and pops the gear shifter position to neutral. He gives it a heave to get it rolling, and watches as the van creeps forward. Entering the back door of his building, Clive turns to see the vehicle with its towering antenna slowly gain momentum, as it rolls down the alleyway.

~*~

Making his way down the hall, Clive approaches his apartment and is greeted by a reporter with a camera crew. "Private Investigator, Clive Wilts..." The reporter then shoves the microphone unceremoniously toward his face.

Clive replies sarcastically. "Nice to meet you, Wilts."

The reporter stares at Clive, confused by the response. "No, no... I'm not Wilts. You are."

"Yes, I am."

Hastily recovering from the wise-cracking introduction, the reporter continues. "Do you, Mister Wilts, have an official comment for News Eleven about the most recent incident with the Santa Monica Sniper?"

Clive puts on an expression of concern and looks past the cameraman toward the alleyway out back. "Eleven...Huh? Is that your news van outside?"

"Yes, and you are Private Investigator, Clive Wilts?"

With a peculiar look on his face, Clive continues to stare over the reporter's shoulder. He leans forward to speak directly into the microphone and asks, "Do you usually drive it down the street with that big antenna-thing up in the air?"

Now it's the reporter's turn to look confused. "No... Why do you ask?"

Clive points outside and innocently comments, "Because it's rolling, and it doesn't look as if anyone is driving."

The reporter's eyes suddenly widen, as one of the camera crew breaks into a run down the hall. Clive pulls out his keys and unlocks his door, as the confused reporter looks around and utters, "Do we keep shooting?"

Clive enters his apartment, pokes his head out momentarily and waves. "For the record, I have no comment." The apartment door slams closed followed by the sound of multiple locks fastening into place.

Chapter 16

The next morning, Clive exits his apartment to find an empty hallway. He stops to listen a moment then mutters to himself, "The reporters are probably gathered outside to mob me..." Locking the door behind him, he is expecting to see the press at any moment as he walks down the hallway. Stepping outside, Clive is met by two police officers flanked by two gentlemen in bargain-warehouse suits. Surprised that there are no cameras or reporters around, the private investigator takes a step back and timidly inquires, "Can I help you fellas?"

"Are you Clive Wilts?"

Clive looks at the uniformed officer, makes note of his badge number and replies. "Sure... And, who are these guys?" One of the police officers circles around behind Clive to block him from returning to the building. The other officer gestures to an unmarked police car. "You need to come with us."

"Do I have a choice?"

Clive looks to the men in suits, and one of them simply states, "Nope."

The police officer standing next to Clive asks, "Want me to put the cuffs on?" The suits both shake their heads and then usher their detainee toward the squad car.

Giving each of the men a good looking over, Clive absentmindedly rubs his wrists at the terrible thought of being handcuffed. "Thanks. I guess..."

~*~

The squad car drives down the street with Clive sandwiched in the back seat between the pair of suited men. Waiting for them to initiate, Clive looks from one to the other and folds his hands on his lap. Finally, he asks, "So, fellas... Where are we headed?"

The police officers in front remain silently staring ahead. One of the suits turns to Clive and speaks. "Unless you start talking, Wilts... You will be arrested and sent off to jail."

"What would you like to talk about?"

"That shooting yesterday..."

Clive looks to each of the men in turn. "I wasn't there." The officers remain silent, frowning, until he reluctantly adds, "What I mean is, I wasn't there when the shooting happened. You see, I heard the shot and arrived shortly after."

"Leaving the scene of a crime is a serious charge."

Clive shifts uneasily in his seat and refolds his hands. "That's not exactly true... I stuck around the crime site, until the whole circus pulled in."

One of the suits takes a police report from the seat-back in front of him, opens the folder and studies it as he replies. "The officer on the scene said that when he looked for you for questioning, you were gone."

"I gave him my name and how to contact me later. Besides, I wasn't even there when the shots were fired, and nobody else was talking, so I know about as much as you."

"What do you know?"

"Not much... How's John?"

"Who?"

"The Meter Maid, uh..., I mean, *the guy*."

"He'll live."

Relieved, Clive nods and responds, "That's good. He's a person who really enjoys his job."

The man holding the folder, sits closer to Clive and presses him further. "What did you say to the crowd before the police arrived on the scene?"

"Nothing... Why?"

The cop with the report looks past Clive to his silent partner and continues. "It seems that two gunshots were fired. A man was wounded, and a wheelie-cart spun out of control. No one saw anything, and everyone turned into brain-dead gawkers by the time we got there to ask any questions."

"That's not too surprising... What...? Did you guys get there about an hour after it happened?"

The silent one thrusts an elbow is into Clive's ribs, and the other one warns, "Cool it with the smart-ass remarks, Wilts, or you'll sit this whole thing out in a jail cell."

"What would that get you?"

"Satisfaction."

"Who'll catch your shooter?"

"We will, sooner or later... We sure don't need some Private Dick bumbling in and taking all the credit."

"I prefer *PI or Private Investigator*." Clive gets the elbow again, and he nods his head in understanding. He looks from one man to the other. Then, he turns and stares ahead, as the car continues to cruise the streets of North Hollywood.

Eventually, the driver looks in the rear-view mirror to see one of the suits make a circular motion with his hand. Relieved that the off-the-record interrogation is almost over, Clive sits silently and waits for his private ride to end. Casually, he steals a glance to the file folder and wonders what information they might possibly have.

The squad car pulls into a prime parking spot in front of the apartment building, and Clive makes a move to get out. When no one budges from their seats to ease his departure, Clive looks at them with uncertainty. "Uhm... This is my stop."

The suit that did all the talking turns to look at Clive, glances at his partner and comments. "If you find anything, you come to the PD first, understand?"

"Sure... I will. I'll put any information in good hands."

"You better..."

"May I go?"

The suit adds, "If we find you're holding out on us, we'll slap you in the tank 'til next Christmas."

Clive counts the months until December and asks, "That's real sweet, guys. This Christmas, or the next one...?" Another sharp elbow juts into his ribs, and Clive winces. Holding back more snarky comments, Clive looks to one, then to the other man flanking him and asks, "Are we done here?"

"We're watching you, Wilts." When the car door opens, the man with the file folder tucks it away and steps out. Following him, Clive quickly scoots along the bench seat and takes a step to the curb, out of arm's reach. He rubs where the other man had repeatedly jabbed his side, groaning, "Thanks... If I need any help, I'll just give a whistle." The plainclothes officer points a warning finger at Clive and climbs back into the unmarked police car.

Standing in front of his apartment building, Clive watches as the car slowly pulls away and then stops at the corner. He waits until the brake lights finally blink off, and the car pulls ahead to make the turn. Gazing down the sidewalk, he notices that there isn't a hint of any news crew in sight. Walking down the block to his car, he murmurs to himself, "Those undercover guys are like the plague... *No one* wants to be around them."

Chapter 17

Clive drives past his regular coffee shop and finds a parking spot not too far from the front door. Poking his head up from the open car roof, he looks around to see if he is being followed. All clear, he gets out and puts on a pair of aviator sunglasses, as if it would disguise him while in his distinct, tropical getup. At the entrance to the shop, Clive checks for followers again, sighs with satisfaction and goes inside.

Waiting at the counter for his order, Clive scans the tables for an abandoned newspaper. A tap on his shoulder nearly makes him jump out of his skin. Spinning, he comes face to face with Maryanne. She laughs and smiles playfully. "Oops… Did I startle you?"

Clive quickly regains his composure and returns the smile. "Uh… Yes, you did. I've been a little on-edge lately."

"I'm sorry."

"There's no need to be sorry. Sometimes my work follows me around."

Her smile broadens. "Yes, I've been reading that."

"In the newspaper…?"

"You're all over the front-page." Less than enthused, Clive grabs his coffee and Danish from the serving counter. Moving in closer, Maryanne leans over and whispers. "Actually, I was worried about you."

Blushing, he can't help but ask, "Yeah...? Why's that?"

"Yours is usually the first friendly face I see each day. When I came in and you weren't here, it felt kind of weird."

Dumbstruck at the candid revelation, Clive utters, "Yeah... I, uh, had some pressing business that took me for a ride this morning."

"Do you want to sit at my table? I'm just over here."

Clive looks to the table with her purse on it, and feels the surge of anxiety prompted by the dream-come-true invitation. "Yeah, sure... If you're not expecting someone else…"

Maryanne goes to her seat. Clive follows behind and sits in the chair across from her. Not knowing what to say, he sips his coffee and takes a large bite of his Danish. His mouth full, he chews slowly while glancing around the coffee shop. There is a folded newspaper, face down, in the middle of the table, and Clive tries his best to avoid staring at it. Maryanne notices and puts on a flirtatious smile. "Aren't you a bit curious?"

Clive nearly chokes on a gulp of coffee. "About you?"

She laughs, thinking he is only kidding with her. "No, Mister Detective… Aren't you curious about what they have to say about you in the newspaper?"

Relieved, he swallows the mouthful, smiles and relaxes. "Sure...What lies are they telling now?" He flips the paper over and unfolds it. Scanning the front-page article and photograph, the grin falls from his face.

Maryanne sees his expression and shows her concern. "It's terrible, huh?"

Clive glances up at her and then continues reading. "Yes… Uh, yes, it is…"

"I can't believe you were actually right there at the scene of the shooting when it all happened."

"I can't either, because I wasn't."

Maryanne looks confused and leans over the table to reexamine the front-page photo. "That's what the article says. They have a remarkable picture of the whole thing right there." With the newspaper laid out on the table, Clive sits back to stare at the front-page photograph. "That's strange…"

"Are you okay?"

Clive shakes off the weird sensation caused by the misleading photo and headline. He looks at Maryanne. "Yeah, I'm fine. Do you think I could keep this newspaper?"

"Sure."

Leaning forward over the enlarged newspaper image, Clive studies it. The details of the shooting are in the write-up, but the perspective of the photograph arouses his suspicions. With a troubled look on his face, he groans softly as he reads. Finally, he folds the paper over and looks back to Maryanne. "I've got to get going. Thanks for the newspaper and the company… It's been nice."

Clive stuffs the rest of the pastry into his mouth, grabs his coffee and heads for the door. Maryanne waves and calls after him. "See you, Magnum!" She watches, as he calmly walks to the door, steps outside, and then suddenly breaks into a run past the front window.

~*~

The car speeds through the streets of North Hollywood toward Clive's office. A block away from his destination, while sitting at a stoplight, Clive looks at the picture-perfect photograph of him at the scene of the most recent shooting. Then, he looks over at his duffle with his camera on the seat.

When the light changes to green, he drives ahead and turns into the parking lot alongside his office building. Instantly, he is met by news crews with microphones and cameras pointed at him. One of the reporters hollers out,

"Detective Wilts! Any strong leads on the shooter's identity? Are you going to wrap this case up soon?"

Clive reaches across the car for the paper and his duffle. He murmurs under his breath. "I *might* be able to work, if you guys could give me a little breathing room." Exiting the car, Clive makes his way past the cameras toward the front of the building. He pulls open one of the front doors and looks back at the news teams. Raising a hand to stop them from following, he pleads, "Please… I don't have anything to give you now."

A reporter and cameraman push their way forward to ask, "Why do you think he's doing it?"

Clive pauses inside the entryway and then turns to the assembly of correspondents. He stares into the clear, round camera lenses. Then, he looks around at all the bright, shining lights and at the horde of microphones pointed directly at him. A realization comes to him, and he simply utters, "Power."

Curious, the news reporter patiently waits for something more and then raises the microphone closer to Clive. "What's that?"

Clive holds the door open and sweeps his pointer finger across the crowd. "He knows that every one of you will run all over town trying to get the best scoop, and that you will practically kill yourselves or others in the process." Standing in the doorway, recalling what John the meter-man said about *power*, he puffs up a bit and continues to address the reporters. "He watches, as you lose all concern for your family, your friends or anyone else in your life. As you become obsessed…. He laughs, as you hassle anyone that might have a bit of a story and beat it, until it no longer resembles a dead horse." Clive's gaze travels over the crowd of reporters, and he makes eye contact with each of them. "The shooter is a news junkie. That's what he feeds on… *That's* what keeps him going. You all know who is ultimately responsible."

Citation for Murder

With a cameraman close behind, another reporter pushes forward and jabs his microphone toward Clive's face. "Detective Wilts... Am I to understand that you think it's *our* fault that he pulls the trigger?"

Tightening his lips, Clive sighs and then responds. "Nope, it's *all* of our faults." He gestures toward the crowd. "Each and every one of us... For always having to know the latest news and see it for ourselves..." He looks directly at the reporter who asked the original question and leans into the mic. "You're just another person loving your work without a care or thought about the consequences to society." On that note, Clive steps inside, pulls the door closed, and hurries up the stairs to his second-floor office.

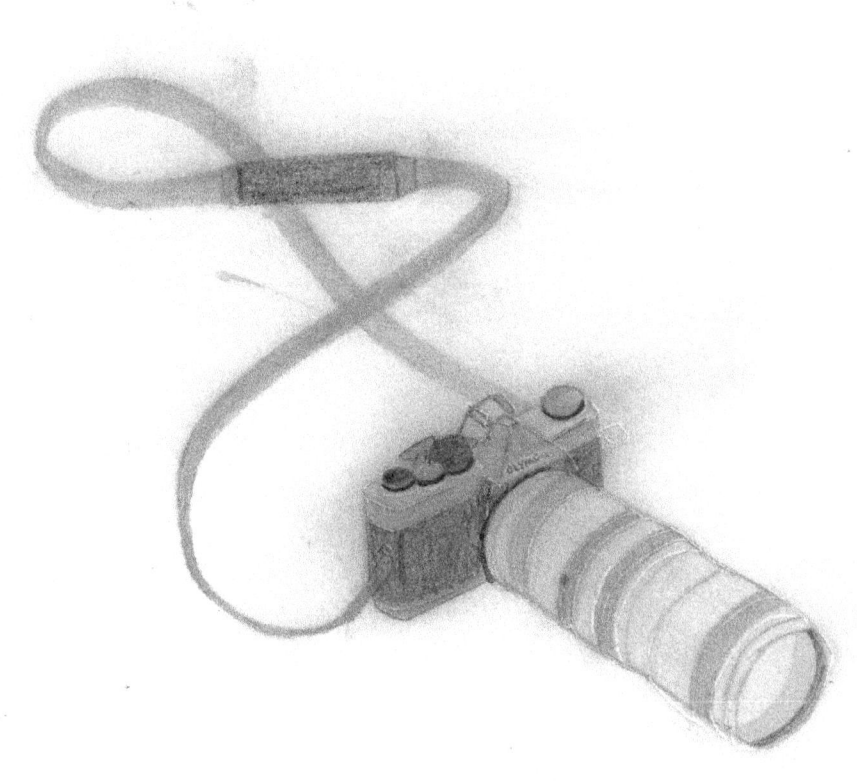

Chapter 18

The front door of the office bursts open, and Clive is greeted by Delores at her desk. "Mr. Wilts, did you see that you're on the front-page of all the papers today?"

After his speech outside, his mood seems to have changed along with his perception. "Yeah… Great photograph, but it's not mine."

She is very surprised. "It isn't?"

As he closes the office door behind him, Clive gives her a funny look and a smile. "My photos are still in the camera. But, it's a really good one, isn't it?"

She watches him merrily trot past her desk to his inner office and flip on the light switch. With a shrug, she responds, "I guess, as far as murder scenes go…"

Standing behind his desk, Clive tosses down the newspaper and turns to the doorway with his camera in hand. Before he has a chance to call out for her, Delores appears at the entry with pen and paper. He looks at her and declares, "*Attempted*-murder scene… That photograph is *too* good!" Clive winds the film in the camera and flips open the back.

Delores comments, "It's not *that* great of a picture. Seems kind of far away…"

"Yeah, and you'll notice that I'm *in* the photo."

"You *are*? If it wasn't you that took it, then who did?"

The secretary watches him remove the roll of film and hold it eagerly in his hand. Nearly bursting with excitement,

Clive explains, "It was a total setup. I arrived on the scene just after the gunshots were fired. There were two or three people who stopped before me, but they didn't approach the wreck." Clive tosses the film to Delores and picks up the newspaper. "Look at that great shot..."

She steps forward for a closer look. "Yes, it was the only thing on the newsstands this morning."

Clive taps his finger on the front-page photo. "Unbelievable!"

Delores shifts the small roll of film to her other hand and replies, "The article says you were the first one at the scene of the crime. Lucky the photographer was in the right spot."

"Luck has got nothing to do with it. He was definitely in the right spot and must've had a hell of a lens on there too. Nobody walks around with a lens that long unless you're a wildlife photographer, or just happens to shoot a photo of a murder scene."

"*Attempted*-murder scene..."

"Yeah... Right..."

"So, you think the photographer is the shooter, too?"

"Or has an inside scoop..."

"Like a tip?"

"Yeah, so they know when and where beforehand."

Delores' face crinkles at the idea. "That's really sick..."

Taking a seat and kicking back, Clive nods. "That's what the whole news media circus does to you these days."

The receptionist looks to the used canister of film held in her hand. "So, did you get a shot of him?"

"I didn't have nearly as good of a lens setup as he did, but I covered the area pretty well. Have them do the normal print processing and get 'em back here as soon as you can." Clive gets up and goes to the window looking over the street.

He peeks through the blinds at the news teams hanging out below and murmurs, "Kill those lights, will ya..."

"Anything else?"

"That's it for now..." Behind him, Delores flips the light switch and swings the door shut as she exits.

~*~

A few blocks in from the Pacific coastline, the rooftop view of the ocean is amazing. A cool breeze blows, rustling the leafy tree limbs that sway alongside the multi-story building. On the tar-sealed rooftop, next to metal boxes containing air conditioning units, a compact suitcase opens to reveal the disassembled parts of a sniper rifle.

Slender hands reach in to take out the two-part polymer stock. Next, the rifle barrel is taken out, lined up with the fore-stock and clicked into place. After a scope is attached, crosshairs slowly scan the city streets below.

~*~

Clive sits in his office and dials the older-model rotary telephone on his desk. After several rings, someone answers. "Santa Monica Police Department, how may I direct your call?"

"Hello. Detective Buckley, please..." The line switches to music, and Clive fiddles with papers on his desk as he waits. Halfway into an REO Speedwagon tune, the phone line clicks again, and the detective answers. "Buckley, here..."

"Yeah, good morning to you too, pal."

"What is it, Clive?"

"I really don't appreciate you sending the goon squad after me this morning. That's the kind of thing that will get the neighbors talking."

Buckley responds with a faraway tone, as if he is on speakerphone or distracted with other things. "Wasn't my call on that one... Some of the higher-ups are none too enthused about you being anywhere near this case."

"Don't tell them yet, but I might have something."

"Yeah? What is it?"

"I'm not sure exactly, and it's nothing solid."

"When will you have something we can use?"

"Possibly later today or tomorrow, but I sure as hell won't be sharing any information if you don't keep those *civets* away from my home and office."

"What's a civet?"

"You have dictionaries over there, don't you? Look it up for yourself." Clive hangs up, leans back in his squeaky chair and puts his feet up. Though satisfied with his progress report, he thinks of another witty comment to toss at the detective and considers calling him back.

There is a soft knock on his office door, and Delores pops her head in. "I have some photos for you, Mr. Wilts."

Excited, Clive tilts his chair forward and motions her in. "Wow, that was really fast."

Delores grins as she approaches. "I think the teenage kid working there has a crush on me. When I tell him ASAP, he drops everything else he's doing to work on my stuff."

Amused, Clive gives her a look. "I'll remember that."

She hands him the envelope of prints. He opens it and immediately begins flipping through the photographs. Curious, Delores leans over his desk to peer at panoramic shots of Santa Monica streets. "That sweet kid likes me a lot, but not enough to pay your tab over there."

Clive glances up at her. "Oh, yeah…" Resting the stack of photos on his lap, Clive takes out the envelope of cash from his pocket, peels off a few twenty dollar bills and slides them across the desk. "See if that will make a dent in our account…"

She counts the money and shrugs. "It's a good start."

Chapter 19

Using the natural light coming in through the windows, Clive sits at his desk studying a series of panoramic photos. The front page of the newspaper is spread open on his lap, and he references the featured image with the assortment of pictures on his desk. He selects one of the photos in the series of shots and holds it up against the newspaper image, trying to visualize the reverse angle.

The phone rings several times, until Delores picks up the call in the outer office. Shortly, there is a knock at his door, and the secretary pokes her head inside Clive's private chamber. "Mister Wilts, there is a *Catherine* on the line. She wants to know if you have any information or pictures for her yet?"

Distracted from his task, he looks at Delores and waves her over. "I'll talk to her in a minute. What do you think?" Selecting two photos, he places them against the newspaper. "Which of these would be the best reverse angle of the front-page photo they have here?"

The receptionist enters the room, moves around the desk and has a look over Clive's shoulder. He holds up one and then the other. She stares at them both a while before pointing to the photo on the left. "I think the first one, taken from up high... The second photograph has a bit of it, though." The private investigator takes out a marker, pulls the cap with his teeth and circles a multi-story, white building that is in both photographs. "You have a good eye. That's exactly what I was thinking, too.

Could you take these negatives down to your special guy-friend and have this portion of the photo blown up at different levels of enlargement?"

She picks up the envelope containing the negatives and takes the two photographs. "How soon do you want them?"

Clive gives her a playful wink. "Depends… How soon can you get them?"

Delores rolls her eyes and walks to the door. "You'll probably have them in half an hour." As she closes the door, she looks back. "Don't forget the lady on the phone."

"Oh yeah…" Then, as he hears Delores getting her purse and keys, Clive hollers after her. "Make the blow-ups doubles!" The front door opens and closes, as Clive grabs the phone. "Private Investigator Wilts here… I'm fine, and how are you?" He strains to listen, as the voice speaks in a hushed tone. Pressing the phone receiver harder against his ear, Clive utters, "I can barely hear you." When the voice repeats a bit louder, Clive answers, "Well, not necessarily… But, I did get a photograph in the direction of where the gunshot came from." He continues to listen, as the voice on the other end of the call gets excited and louder. Nodding his head, he switches the phone to his other ear. "Okay… Give me an hour at least. If I'm not here, I'll leave the photographs with my receptionist… Okay, we'll see." Hanging up the phone, he looks again at the newspaper's front-page picture. He murmurs to himself, "Damn, that's a thin lead you have, Clive. Very thin…"

~*~

As he returns from the bathroom down the hall, Clive sees someone waiting at the door of his detective agency. Approaching, he notices that it's a leather-clad motorcycle messenger with a pouch over his shoulder. After glancing at his watch, Clive clears his throat to get the messenger's attention. "Excuse me… Can I help you?"

Citation for Murder

The messenger regards the odd-looking character in the Hawaiian shirt and hooks a thumb to the detective agency door. "Yeah, I'm supposed to pick something up here."

"What are you picking up?"

"Do you work here?"

"Yes, I do."

The messenger looks at the order ticket and replies, "Says here, I'm to pick up an envelope or a package."

Clive sighs and moves past the messenger to unlock the door. "Yeah, I figured it was something like that."

"Are you Wilts?"

"Maybe…" Clive opens the door, and the messenger follows him into the office. "Who are you picking up for?"

"Let's see… I was sent to pick up this package for a…" The messenger looks at the slip of paper and tucks it away in his pocket again. "…Catherine." Clive gestures to one of the waiting room chairs and proceeds toward his private office. "Have a seat… You're a bit early…"

Just as Clive is about to close the door to his own office, the agency's front door opens again and Delores steps inside. Clive moves to meet her at her desk and gives her a suggestive look. "Now, that was *really* fast!"

She smiles gamely, fixes her hair, and gives him the envelope with the enlargements. "The cash on hand helped. Anything else, Mister Wilts?"

Across the room, the messenger zips up his jacket, stands and adjusts his shoulder bag. Clive looks past Delores and ushers the messenger to sit back down. "Hold on there, buddy. This package won't be ready for some time."

"How long?"

Clive peeks in the large envelope, looks at his watch and grunts, "Could be quite a while… I told her *about an hour.*"

With a shrug, the courier sits and replies, "I'm on the clock and was told to wait however long it takes."

"Good… I have to sort through this and put it together. Until it's ready, Miss Snowder will entertain you with bad jokes and dancing." He winks good-humoredly at Delores, who merely rolls her eyes at him. Clive hears the unzipping of a motorcycle jacket as, clutching the enlargements, he scoots off to his office and shuts the door behind him.

Chapter 20

The photographic enlargements are spread out on the desk. Clive leans over to closely examine the details. He lifts one up, sits in his chair and reaches over to pull open a desk drawer. After shuffling through the contents, he pulls out a magnifying glass and holds it over the photo. "Holy crap..."

He puts the enlargement back on the desk, opens another drawer and takes out a sheet of transparency plastic. He tapes the clear sheet over the photograph, grabs a marker and circles a silhouette on the rooftop of one of the buildings. Clive places a sticky note on the plastic covering, jots down a short message and slides the photo into a manila envelope. Using the marker, he writes Catherine's name across the front of the packet.

Clive lifts the phone and pushes the intercom button. "Delores, can you please see me in my office?"

In a moment, she opens his office door and peeks in. "Yes, Mister Wilts?"

Clive urgently waves her in, and she closes the door behind her. When she comes over to his desk, Clive hands her one of the unmarked enlargements. "Can you see anything?"

Delores studies the photograph and points to the rooftop of the white building. "Looks like you might have the photographer on the rooftop."

He hands her the magnifying glass, pushes back in his chair and confidently comments, "We'll call him *the shooter*."

Narrowing her eyes to squint, the secretary studies the tiny, distorted image under the lens of the magnifying glass. "Hmm, I don't know…"

"He's holding the gun."

"Are you sure that's a rifle?"

"I guess it could be a broom for sweeping that roof ledge. It's not a camera, at least."

Delores is not sure if a rifle is too far of a stretch, but she nods her head in agreement. "No, it's probably not a camera… Do you think he also took the photo of the crime scene?"

"The reverse photo was taken just before I got my camera out to snap these shots, so it must be him." Clive leans forward to study the details of the enlarged picture again. "And, I doubt anyone else could have gotten there that quick."

Delores hands back the photo and the magnifying glass. She leans her hip on the edge of the desktop and thinks aloud, "Then, why is he still holding that rifle… or whatever it is?" Concerned, she looks at Clive.

With a troubled expression, Clive puts the enlargement down on the desk and softly replies, "Yeah… The mere thought of it scares the crap out of me, too. He's either posing with the sniper rifle or setting up for another shot that he didn't take." The private investigator taps the package he put together for Catherine and looks to Delores. "I'll need you to distract that motorcycle messenger a bit longer. This information needs to get to Buckley before anyone else sees it, or my ass is toast." Delores nods her head in agreement and takes the envelope. She watches, as Clive puts several of the photo doubles into another envelope and then jots a short note on a piece of paper. He passes the message to Delores and instructs, "After I leave, give Buckley a call and tell him to meet me at that address in

Santa Monica. Tell him it's important he doesn't *miss the boat*." Clive looks at his watch. "If I don't call you here by... Let's say, two-thirty, then give the messenger the envelope."

She looks at the address on the slip of paper and judges the driving distance while mentally calculating time in traffic. "Does that give you enough time to get this to Buckley first?" Clive shrugs uncertain. "It should, I think. And, be *sure* to tell him *not to miss the boat this time!*"

"Is that a joke or something?"

"He'll understand." Clive puts his camera in the bag, slings it over his shoulder, and grabs the newspaper along with the enlargements. "I'm off. Wish me luck."

"Luck..." Following him out, Delores watches Clive give a hurried wave while hustling past the leather-clad rider.

The messenger stands and starts to zip his jacket again. At the door, Clive turns to him and gestures to his secretary. "The package you're to deliver won't be ready for some time. Miss Snowder will take care of you." Without another word, Clive slips out into the empty hallway and runs to the stairs, leaving the receptionist to the task of delaying the delivery. Unfazed, she pulls Clive's office door closed with a gentle click, smiles sweetly at the messenger, and then leans on her desk. "Right...Where were we?" The jacket creaks and then unzips.

~*~

Heading toward Santa Monica, the little red sports car races down the freeway. On his way to the location of the latest shooting, weaving in and out of afternoon traffic, Clive is determined to deliver his information to Detective Buckley before time runs out.

Chapter 21

Clive drives up to the white building identified in the photo enlargement and finds an open parking spot along the street. He scrutinizes the area and determines that the building is a full block and a half from the location of the recent shooting. After grabbing the newspaper and photos from the passenger seat, he steps out and walks around the car to feed the meter. He stares at the flashing red light next to the *expired* message and briefly considers not paying it.

While approaching the gated entrance of the multi-story residential building, Clive notices the meager attempt at security and mutters, "Sometimes I wonder why they even bother to try." His finger presses each apartment's buzzer, and then he looks out into the street as he waits. After a moment, the button for apartment eighteen lights up, and a voice crackles through the intercom. "Hello… Who is it? Hello…?" Clive puts his hand over his mouth and speaks through his fingers to muffle his voice. "Hello, I have a delivery for apartment…" With a click, the lock on the gate buzzes open, and Clive steps inside to head down the first-floor hallway.

At the end of the corridor, Clive arrives at a wide, tiled staircase. Looking back toward the entry, he grumbles, "What… No elevator?" For a moment, he stares at the stairway. He looks upward at the winding route to the floors above, and then begrudgingly begins to climb.

~*~

Huffing and puffing, Clive comes up the last set of stairs to arrive at the fifth floor. Sweating and breathing hard, he stops to rest and leans on the railing. Placing a foot on the top stair tread, he gazes down the hall and tries to locate which doorway would give him rooftop access.

Midway down the corridor, Clive stops at a plain, wooden door with no apartment number on it. Pulling the door open, he is presented with yet another set of stairs leading upward. He looks to the old, metal door at the top and spots a shiny new padlock on the rusty hasp.

Perspiration drips from his brow, as Clive trudges up the remaining stairs. The private investigator reaches the top and fans his coat by the lapels to cool off. Pushing on the heavy door, Clive hears the metal hasp rattle against the padlock. Unimpressed with another poor attempt at security, he takes a lock-picking set from his pocket and goes to work on it.

~*~

When the rooftop access door pushes open, Clive steps out and looks around. Just a standard, hot-tarred roof with rattling air-conditioner units and old antennas fastened to it. Clive jumps slightly, when the door behind him swings shut with a scraping-bang. He makes his way over to the low, parapet wall surrounding the rooftop's edge and peers over. Below, Clive sees the top of Detective Buckley's head waiting by the gated entrance. Cupping his hands around his mouth, he calls out, "Hey, Buckley... Up here!"

The detective takes a few steps back from the building and looks up. He sees Clive waving at him and hollers back. "What the hell are you doing up there?"

"Come on up, and I'll show you."

Buckley looks at the security gate in front of him and then back up to the rooftop. He shakes his head and grumbles, "This better be good, Wilts."

On the roof, Clive surveys the view of the surrounding buildings and holds the newspaper out at arm's length to compare the vantage point with the front-page photograph. The sound of the rooftop access door creaking open turns Clive around, and he sees Buckley step out. The police detective wipes away the sweat glistening on his forehead, heaves his chest to catch his breath and then calls out to Clive. "Damn you, Wilts! Why in heck did you get me up here?"

Clive lowers the newspaper and motions him over. "Buckley! Take a look at this." The police detective comes over, glances at the front-page newspaper headline and grouses. "I've already seen today's paper."

Clive puts the paper aside and takes out the enlargement of the photograph he took at the scene of the latest occurrence. He hands it over to Buckley. "What do you think of this?"

The detective takes the photo enlargement from Clive, studies it for a second and then looks up with a disgusted expression on his face. "What the heck am I looking at here?" The private investigator offers Buckley the magnifying glass and points to the roofline of the building they are standing on. "Here, use this."

Appraising it again, Buckley shakes his head, baffled. "Clive, I don't see it." Clive points to the figure in the photo. The detective stares at it for a few seconds and grumbles, "That's great... You want me to put it out on the police wire that we're looking for a dark spec of something that's holding some unidentifiable thing?" Handing the photo and magnifying glass back to Clive, he groans, "I don't know what the hell's wrong with you. You call me out here to trespass and then show me a crappy photo that could be anything...? By the way, your secretary's boat joke was uncalled for."

"How closely did you look at the paper today?"

Buckley's irritation mounts, and he is ready to storm away. "Well-enough to see your dumb-ass is in it again!"

Not even slightly offended by the rude comment, Clive responds. "As a decoy, remember? So that your guys can swoop in to catch the shooter." Clive waits for his remark to have its effect and then adds, "You know, I think I've been doing my part in this very well." He unfolds the newspaper, hands it over to Buckley and points to the photo on the front. "Take another look at it." Clive steps out of the way, so Buckley has the same exact perspective as the picture's photographer.

The detective glances at the front-page image and then looks down the street to the location of the most recent attack. He does a double-take and then turns to Clive questioningly. "Who took this photo?"

"Who do you think?"

"You're implying that the actual shooter took a picture of the crime scene?"

"That, or someone really close by…"

Buckley looks at the newspaper photo again, and Clive hands him the enlargement of the reverse angle to compare it. It only takes Buckley a second to make the connection between the two. "And, you took this shot?"

"Yep."

"When?"

"Right after I arrived on the scene."

"As soon as you got there?"

"Maybe a minute later… I checked the victim's pulse first and found that he was still alive."

"How long was it from the time you heard gunshots to the time you snapped this?"

"Three minutes, tops."

Buckley holds the newspaper in one hand and the enlargement in the other, considering the timing of the shots.

He looks back to the stairway door, thinks about the climb up, and comments to Clive. "Keep this information to yourself, until I have the crime unit take a look at it." Unable to hide a telling expression, Clive turns away, and Buckley immediately knows that something is up. Annoyed, the detective tilts his head and bluntly asks, "Who else has seen this photo?"

"Well, only me and Delores, so far…"

"What do you mean, *so far*? Until we can track this rooftop photographer down, I don't want this out to anyone."

Clive peeks at his watch, pulls out his phone and flips it open. "It's supposed to go out to one of my clients soon."

"What?!?"

"Hey, I showed you first!" Lifting his phone in the air, he waves it around, trying to get reception.

Buckley barks angrily. "Dammit! Call your secretary right now and tell her to hold onto that photo!"

Clive steps away, continuing to wave the phone high in the air, looking for any hint of a connection. "What do you think I'm trying to do?"

Buckley pats his pockets and starts for the doorway. "My phone is in the car. Come on." Clive follows toward the stairs with his arm waving in the air, still trying to get his mobile phone to work.

Chapter 22

Buckley and Clive burst from the gated doors of the apartment building, out of breath and gleaming with sweat. They race to a nondescript sedan parked beside a red-painted curb, and Buckley pulls the door open to grab his cell phone from inside. He hits redial, tosses the phone to Clive and urgently adds, "Make sure she doesn't let that photo out!"

Clive hears the ring tone, as he wipes the perspiration from his brow. The phone rings several times, and Clive peers at his own phone to see that he still doesn't have reception. Delores finally picks up. "Clive Wilts, the Private Investigator: *You lost it, and he'll find it.*"

"Is that how you usually answer the phone?"

"Uh, Mister Wilts?"

Clive looks over to see the urgency on Buckley's face. "Yes, hello Delores, I need you to hold on to that package for Catherine... Oh..." He glances at Buckley and pivots away. "Okay, sure... No, nothing else... I'll see you tomorrow."

The police detective moves closer, trying to overhear. Clive ends the call and tosses the cell phone back to Buckley. He catches it and asks, "Did she hold onto it?"

"No, it's gone."

"Dammit, Wilts! To who?"

"A client."

"What client?"

Clive takes a step back, as Buckley's features begin to turn red. "My clients, who pay their bills, are confidential."

Buckley turns toward his car and throws his phone inside. "Damn it!!!" He slams the passenger door shut and pounds his fist on the roof. "Wilts, if you screw this up for us, I'm gonna lock you up and bury your personnel file so deep, it'll take the world a week to hear you fart!"

Clive adjusts his collar and protests. "Hold it, Buckley. I'm giving you the tip, and I expect the commission for it, too." Clive continues, as Buckley moves around to the driver's side and opens the car door. "Why don't you pull your panties out of your crack and get your best guys on this right away? Besides, I doubt it will even go public."

Getting into the car, Buckley looks to the windshield and sees a citation tucked under the driver's side wiper blade. He reaches out and around, tears the parking ticket from the window and tosses it away. As Clive cracks a smile and tries to hide his amusement, Buckley directs a pointed finger at him. "Don't you say a damn word!" He tosses Clive's newspaper and photo enlargement to the passenger-side seat and barks, "I'm keeping those."

"No problem, Buckley… Could I get a receipt for them?" Without answering, the police detective slams his car door and turns the ignition. Clive steps over and leans down to speak through the open window. "I'll just send you an invoice…" Buckley pounds on the gas pedal and peels out into the street. Clive waves after him and calls out, "See you later…"

The crumpled parking ticket blows to the curb, and Clive lets out a giggle as he moves down the street. At his car, he turns back and glances up to the top of the white building. Briefly, he thinks he sees someone watching and duck back. Then he relaxes, assuming that it is probably just one of the many rooftop antennas.

Citation for Murder

~*~

The lingering glow of evening light filters through the palm fronds on the trees outside Clive's apartment windows. He slouches back on his couch, as he reads a glossy issue of *Popular Investigator Magazine*. He takes a long sip of a Michelob, flips a page and reaches over to set his beer down on the table. The phone rings, and he glances at his wristwatch before lifting the receiver from the cradle to answer. "Hello? Hey, Delores…" After listening to the voice on the other end, Clive responds. "No, I haven't seen the news. Her name is Catherine… McCormick? I don't know. Could be…" Shock suddenly hits, and he drops the magazine to his lap. "No! Really? Oh shit!!!" Sitting up, Clive reaches for the television controller and turns on the TV. "Okay, talk to you later…" He hangs up the phone, tosses the magazine aside and flips through stations until the news show *Inside California* pops up on the screen.

An attractive newscaster addresses the studio camera. "Yes, we're going to display that exclusive photo once again. The very first picture of the *Santa Monica Sniper*, obtained just moments ago by our own special-investigative reporter, Catherine McCormick…"

A professional headshot of Catherine pops up in the corner of the newscast. Putting his head down in his hands, Clive tugs at his thinning hair. "Son of a …"

The home phone rings again, and Clive reaches over to get it but stops short. He looks to the television and his stomach turns when he sees his *shooter photo* plastered across the screen. He hears the newscaster remark, "And, here it is again, folks. The first photograph of the *Santa Monica Sniper*, just after…" The telephone continues to ring, until the answering machine in the kitchen kicks on.

Following the recorded greeting, the angry voice of Detective Buckley screams loud and clear from the other room.

"Wilts, you dumb #%@*! What the hell's wrong with you? Selling that photo to someone in the media?!? I know you're listening, dammit..." Wincing, Clive turns up the volume of the television to drown out the remainder of the message. "Reporting from the streets of Santa Monica is our own Catherine McCormick..."

When Clive sees his client and a camera crew in front of the building in his photograph, he lets out a troubled sigh and clicks the television off. He grabs his drink from the table, downs the rest, tosses the empty aside and, with a whimper, lies back on the couch.

Chapter 23

A new day has dawned. Clive peeks out the front door of his apartment and checks for reporters in the empty hallway. Everything looks clear, so he slips down the back stairs, exits the building and scans the alleyway for any press crews. Hustling around the corner, he makes his way down the street and gets into his car without incident.

Clive fumbles with his keys and looks to his rearview mirror. He is relieved to see no one is following. The car starts, and he shifts into gear. He cranks the wheel, slowly pulls out of the parking spot, hits the gas and zooms down the street.

~*~

Clive slows his car in front of the coffee shop, as he comes up on an unmarked police vehicle with two plain-clothes officers inside. Holding back, Clive rolls past as a delivery truck pulls up beside them and blocks their view of the street. Unnoticed, he presses on the gas pedal and cruises away.

~*~

The street in front of Clive's office building is cluttered with television crews from every channel and vans parked with their broadcasting antennas extended. Clive hunkers down, peering out the window, as he slips past the media circus. Pulling around the block, he finds parking down the street.

Clive checks his side mirrors to see that he hasn't been followed and then takes out his cell phone. He flips it open and punches in his office number. When the phone rings, Delores picks up and Clive whispers, "Hello, Delores? Hi... No... You're right, the place is swarming with media. Did the cops show up yet?" When a car drives past, Clive keeps his voice low, and he sinks further down in the seat. "Okay, that's fine. Did you happen to find anything about where that photograph came from?" He looks around cautiously, listens a moment, and then exclaims, "You did... *Really!?!* Well, yes! Give me the name and address."

Clive opens the glovebox to get a pen and notepad out. He places the pad of paper on his knee and is ready to write. "Okay, go ahead.... Timothy Gustavo... *G-u-s-t-a-v-o*? Okay. He lets people call him *Timmy*? Yeah... What's the address?" After scribbling the address down, Clive reads it silently and taps his pen on the pad. "Yeah, I got it. This might be the thing to keep my ass out of lockup. Thanks, Delores. Call you later." He looks down at the address again, tosses the notebook to the passenger seat and starts the engine. "Hot dog... I'm coming to give you a visit, Timmy." The car pulls out into the street and races through a yellow traffic light.

~*~

The rush-hour traffic on the freeway to Santa Monica is almost at a complete standstill. Clive swerves his car to the shoulder of the road, drives ahead and takes the first exit. Behind several idling cars, he knits his eyebrows and waits for a traffic light to change.

The line of cars finally starts to move forward, and Clive takes a left turn to cross underneath the traffic-packed freeway. He glances at the address scribbled on his note pad and looks down at his *Thomas Guide* map of Los Angeles. Flipping a page on the thick binder, he takes the next right and drives down a street lined with industrial buildings.

A few minutes later, he arrives at a storage unit complex with a sign across the building that reads *Public U' Store-It.*

Clive looks through the open T-tops to the neon signage and verifies the address once again. With a rev of the engine, the little red sports car pulls in and parks by the door to the office. Clive steps out, puts on his jacket and goes inside.

At the front counter, Clive fiddles with a rotating brochure stand until it wobbles and falls behind the check-out. He peers over the counter at the tumbled display, and then pretends not to notice as the clerk, adjusting his pants, comes out from the back. The attendant looks at the dumped rack, shakes his head and kicks it aside to step behind the desk. "What can I help you with?"

"I would like to check out a storage unit."

"How big do you need?"

Clive opens one of the remaining brochures still on the counter and studies the storage sizing chart. "I'm not sure. Could I go inside and take a look at some of them?" The clerk turns to the computer at the desk and uses the mouse to click on a few icons. He waits for the computer to start up and asks, "How many rooms?"

"How many rooms, what?"

The clerk rolls his eyes and clicks the mouse several more times, as he shifts it back and forth. "What, exactly, are you going to be storing?"

Clive turns from the counter to look out the window, and his eyes linger on his sports car. "I'm looking for something that will, uh, maybe fit a Fiero."

The clerk looks up from the computer screen, follows Clive's gaze outside, and sees the small two-seater parked out front. Unimpressed, he sniffs and, in a condescending tone, remarks, "Well, you won't need a big one, then." The printer begins to hum. The clerk waits and then rips off a sheet of paper with a map on it. He tears away the perforated edges and slides it across the counter to Clive. "Here is a map of available units."

He circles a column along the side that lists the various sizes. "And, here are the sizes." The clerk points to the numbers on the different floor levels. "Follow the map and have a look. Then, come back here, and let me know what works for you. Make *sure* you come by here again when you're done, so I can check you out."

Clive takes the map and smiles. "Thanks for your help. I'll have a look-see." As he exits, Clive turns and looks back. "Excuse me... Can I just drive my car up there?"

The clerk glances out the side window at a concrete ramp leading up to storage units arranged in the style of a parking garage. His flaccid features mask his irritation, and he responds, "That's what it's *made* for, unless you *want* to walk."

Chapter 24

The sports car motors up the long, steep ramp to the second floor of the storage complex. The car creaks to a stop and waits as a gate arm lifts open. A surveillance camera is mounted on the wall above and, after waving to the lens, Clive continues driving up the ramp to the next floor. Leveling out at the top, he arrives at a seemingly endless hallway of storage unit doors.

Remembering that there was a unit number included with the address, Clive reaches for the notebook on the passenger seat. Holding his notepad and the storage unit map, he cruises slowly down the corridor, checking the numbers as he goes. The size chart on the map shows the larger units to be farther down, and the address number correlates.

After driving down several lengthy hallways, tires squeaking with each sharp turn, Clive arrives at Timothy's storage unit. He pulls beyond it and parks in front of the next garage door. Clive studies the map for available units in the area and peers around for security cameras pointed his way. The car door swings open, and Clive steps out to have a look down the hall. All is quiet in the complex.

Just to the rear of Clive's car, Timothy's storage unit has a padlock hanging from the latch on the roll-up security door. Taking a knee, Clive pulls out his lock-pick and goes to work. The thin metal picks twist inside the keyhole until, suddenly, the lock releases and pops open. Clive looks over his shoulder, gauging the surrounding silence. He lifts the padlock from the slide, moves the latch aside and raises the roll-up garage door. The sight of the jam-packed contents of the storage unit makes Clive take a step back and mutter aloud, "Holy crap…"

The garage door barely clears a mass of boxes, furniture, and other odd items clustered together. Clive stares, mystified, at the entangled mess. "Timothy Gustavo, *you* are a *pack rat*." Now that he has the unit open, he takes a moment to assess what to do next.

Suddenly, Clive hears the soft squeal of tires on the slick cement floor. At the end of the hallway, the storage clerk, driving a golf cart patrol vehicle, races around the corner. Before the cart even has a chance to come to a complete stop, the clerk yells at Clive. "Hey, bud! You're on the wrong floor."

With an innocent look of confusion, the private investigator turns to face him and remarks, "This one is full."

Pulling up beside Clive, the clerk looks at him like he's nuts. "What's up with you? This one isn't on the list."

Continuing to play the dumb card, Clive looks at the map printout, turns it upside down and then shakes his head. "It looks like it's already being used."

The clerk hops out of the cart, hustles over and pulls the door down. He looks at the open padlock hanging on the slide and turns to Clive. "Was it unlocked?"

"I just opened the door."

"There is a lock on it."

"Sure, but I don't have the key."

"It wasn't locked?

"I guess not."

The storage clerk slides the latch, puts the padlock back through it and clicks it shut. Hopping back into his patrol cart, he grumbles to Clive. "I didn't see you pass the camera that leads to the third floor, so I figured you were probably lost."

Clive turns in a circle, looks around blankly, and acts the part of a misguided customer. "All these halls look the same."

The clerk starts the electric cart, backs up to turn around, and waves him along. "Follow me, I'll show you the spaces."

Opening his car door, Clive hesitates and looks to the other units in the corridor. "Do you have any on this floor?"

"These are the bigger ones. If you're just going to park that dinky car in there, you won't need one like this."

"I think I want one more like this size."

The clerk stops the cart, rolls his eyes and groans. "Okay... Follow me down to the office again, and I'll pull up some other numbers for you."

~*~

In the storage facility office, the clerk stands behind the desk and types at the computer. He notices a car pass the second-floor security camera, observes it for a moment and then grumbles, "Damn, that was close."

Clive leans over the counter and curiously looks to the surveillance camera. "What was close?"

The clerk taps the screen of the monitor. "That guy is in and out of here every other day."

"Yeah? Really...?"

"The ones that come in and out all the time occasionally forget about locking their unit door when they leave. Weirdos... I have to put up with an ass-full of crap if their stuff looks like it's been messed with."

The clerk prints out another map, and Clive tries to remain calm as he watches the vehicle on the security monitor turn at the end of the hallway. "Was that guy in here recently?"

"Yeah, just yesterday... He must have left his lock off.

Clive nods, "Yeah. Must have..."

"Glad we caught it before he freaked." The clerk places the newly printed map on the counter and points to the units.

"Here… Go take a look at these. They're all the biggest ones, and they're on the second floor."

Clive eagerly grabs the map and dashes for the door. "Thanks!"

Chapter 25

Back in his car, Clive zooms up the concrete ramp while pulling his camera from the bag on the seat. Turning at the top, he drives down the long passageway. Garage door after garage door flashes by, as he adjusts the long lens on his camera. Making the last tight turn, he sees, midway down the corridor, the front grill of the white SUV with a bucking horse emblem, they had seen on the security monitor.

Clive lifts the camera from his lap, points it through the windshield and clicks a few shots of the stopped vehicle. "Smile..." He slowly drives nearer and clicks-off several more. "What are you doing, Mr. Gustavo?" Timothy moves alongside the all-terrain vehicle. Clive can see him unloading gear and packing it into the already overstuffed storage unit. He holds the camera and waits for a clean shot of the driver.

With the last of his items packed into the unit, Timothy turns to see Clive driving toward him with a camera pointed in his direction. The little red sports car rolls to a stop, and both parties freeze for a moment, their gazes locked on each other. Clive breaks the stalemate by clicking-off several more photos.

"Yeah... Right there is good, Timmy."

Timothy turns to look at the items positioned at the front of his locker and back to the man in the sports car. Quickly, he pulls down the door and secures the padlock. Clive opens his car door, gets out and approaches. Timothy goes to the driver's side of his vehicle and calls out, "What's the idea, buddy? Why'd you take my picture?"

Pulling his wallet from his back pocket, Clive flips it open to flash his PI identification and then tucks it away. "Mister Gustavo, I have a few questions for you."

With a hint of recognition, Timothy looks Clive over. "You're not a cop. I think I know who you are..."

"I'll ask the questions here. Could you open that storage unit for me again? You have some explaining to do."

Timothy glances at the padlock and then back to Clive, taking a moment, but finally identifying him. "You're that joke of a private investigator, *Wilts PI!*"

In one swift movement, Timothy swings the SUV's door open and jumps into the driver's seat. Clive runs to the other side of the vehicle, snaps a photo, and reaches inside the open window to unlock the door. Hiding his face, Timothy kicks out at the passenger-side door, opening it and smashing it into Clive's chest. With a loud metallic bang, Clive flies back against a storage unit door, almost dropping his camera.

Immediately, Timothy cranks the ignition and slams the vehicle into reverse. Clive presses himself flat against the wall, as the SUV screeches its tires, racing backwards. Abruptly, halfway down the corridor, the unlatched passenger door swings open again and catches on a cement column between the storage units. The vehicle's door is bent back on its hinges and gets flattened-out on the front fender. Clive's jaw drops, and he gasps, "Holy crap...!"

The vehicle stops momentarily, and Clive, following at a jog, lifts his camera to snap a few more shots. The angry driver jumps out, goes around front and gives the passenger-side door a violent kick to bring it back into place. Another forceful kick swings it mostly closed, followed by another to latch it. As he approaches, Clive yells to Timothy. "Hold on there a minute... I have some questions to ask you!"

Timothy gives him the finger and jumps back in the SUV. With tires squealing, the vehicle takes off backwards down the hallway. Pausing to catch his breath, Clive shouts, *"Stop, dammit!"* As the fleeing suspect weaves in reverse down the narrow corridor, Clive shakes his head and mutters, "C'mon, Timmy... *Please* don't make me chase you for this..." At the end of the hallway, the SUV slams into the storage unit directly behind the T-intersection, and Clive sees the driver crank the steering wheel to make it around the tight corner. Clive dashes back to his car, hops inside, starts it and looks up just as the fleeing vehicle pulls away and out of view. "Damn... Buckley is not going to believe this!" Clive shifts into gear, hammers on the gas pedal, and the spinning tires squeal on the slick cement floor.

Chapter 26

At the end of the corridor, Clive spins the steering wheel, makes the turn, and barely misses the smashed garage doors. Accelerating, he narrows the gap between himself and the fleeing suspect. Sounds of racing engines echo off metal storage unit doors, as the vehicles whiz past. Continuing down the next hallway, the white SUV makes a sharp turn, screeching its tires and scraping around the corner. Following with a drifting skid, Clive sees his side mirror come dangerously close to being clipped off, as he narrowly misses trading paint with the unforgiving cinder-block corner. "Son of a ..."

The sports car makes the sharp turn and slides to a halt. Then, Clive hammers on the gas again, attempting to catch up. After a near miss on another treacherous turn, the two vehicles, now almost bumper-to-bumper, race down the corridor.

When the leading vehicle suddenly slams on the brakes, Clive instantly does the same, stopping within inches of the bumper ahead. At the facility entrance, the clerk, in his patrol cart, blocks the exit. Waving away the smell of burnt rubber, the clerk hangs out the side of his cart to yell at the drivers, "Hey, you guys! You can't be racing around in here!"

The sports car's door swings open, and Clive pokes his head out. The larger vehicle ahead hits the gas and takes off. Clive ducks back behind his steering wheel, as the clerk tries to pull out of the way. The SUV smashes past, spinning the small cart on its tiny tires. "Timmy! Not cool..."

Clive pulls his door shut, slams the car in gear, hits the gas and follows. As he zooms by, he waves to the storage clerk, who screams after them. "Slow down, assholes!!!"

The SUV shoots down the ramp and levels out on the parking lot in a shower of sparks. A hard turn skids him across the fenced lot toward the nearest street exit. Clive races down the steep cement ramp and slides to a tire-skidding halt just before the precipitous angle at the bottom. Slowly, he eases off the ramp so as to not damage his low-profile frame, and watches as the fleeing vehicle pulls into street traffic. Clear of the access ramp, Clive floors it and races across the parking lot.

Turning onto the street, Clive spots the SUV, a block ahead, swerving around cars like it's in an auto-theft video game. He stomps his foot down and zips through traffic using the left turn lanes and road shoulders to maneuver his pursuit. Nearly caught up, Clive sees Timothy race through a red light. As he sticks close, he presses on his pathetic horn with a *beeeeeeeeeeeeeeeeeeeeeeeeeep,* creating a wake of confused drivers. "Get out of the way…!"

Clive mops beads of sweat from his forehead, as he continues this dangerous chase. Suddenly, the cell phone in his pocket begins to vibrate and ring. While racing through the busy streets, he fumbles it out and flips it open to answer as calmly as he can. "Hello… Hey, Delores, I'm kinda busy. What…? Another one? Was anyone killed? Crap… Hold on…" Clive veers around a line of stopped cars, following the fleeing vehicle as it swings over into the oncoming lane of traffic, cruises through the intersection and then turns left.

With the mobile phone held to his ear, Clive drives one-handed while he continues to speak. "Yeah, Delores, I'm still here…" Clive flips his blinker, swerves around another car and races onward. "I'm actually tailing Mr. Gustavo right now…" Several cars screech to a halt, honking as Clive races past.

"Yeah... I think he probably knows that I'm following him. Where's a cop when you actually need one? I thought they were supposed to be watching me closely... For Pete's sake, I'd even settle for a Meter Maid's help right now!"

Ahead, the speeding vehicle swings all the way around a turn-about and then drives furiously in the opposite direction. Clive follows the reckless route and narrowly misses a fully loaded landscaping truck. He waves to the three men inside the cab and yells, "Lo siento, amigos!" The truck slams to a stop, and Clive whizzes past, continuing the chase. Still driving one-handed, he comments into the cell phone. "Not you Delores... That was meant for some turf-tenders." He weaves around a line of cars that have pulled aside to avoid the car chase and continues speaking. "Gustavo *has* to be the guy. He's giving me one hell of a chase."

Out of the corner of his eye, Clive spots a black and white police cruiser parked in front of a Winchell's Donut House. With a high-pitched *beeeeeeeeeep*, he lays on his clownish-sounding horn, and waves his cell phone out through the roof as he races by. Just stepping outside with a bakery box, a pair of officers stare, slack-jawed, as the red sports car rips past.

Clive brings his arm back inside the car and continues his phone conversation with Delores. "I just signaled a cop... Yeah, he better be the one, or I'll be on vacation in the county lockup for a while. Please call Detective Buckley, and tell him I need some backup. And this time, don't mention the boat..."

There is an abrupt silence on the line, and Clive realizes the call has dropped. He glances at the display and isn't sure where the conversation was cut off. The small screen shows the icon for no reception, and he groans at the familiar sight. Tossing the device aside, he grips both hands on the wheel and focuses ahead.

In the rear-view mirror, bright flashing lights catch his eye, and Clive turns to see that the police car has joined in the pursuit. The siren blips, and cars ahead of them begin to peel aside to let the speeding vehicles pass by. Signs for *I-10 Freeway* appear, and Clive shakes his head, unhappily muttering, "No… Please, *not the freeway.*"

The SUV hits the brakes, swerves around another car and swings onto the freeway entrance ramp, racing upward along the carpool lane. Clive pounds on the gas pedal and reluctantly follows him around the line of cars. He briefly looks at the rearview mirror to see the police car, with every light flashing, close behind.

Chapter 27

It is rush hour on the I-10 freeway. Trying to lose the tail as it increases in size, the fleeing suspect cuts across lanes of traffic. Clive swerves around the slower moving cars and glances at his mirrors to see several more police vehicles join the chase. "Alright! Here comes the cavalry!" Clive glances to his gas gauge, sees that he still has half a tank and takes a breath. "We're committed. No quitting now, Timmy…"

The line of cars in the chase moves to the left-hand lane, heading east toward the center of Los Angeles. As the traffic ahead of them splits like the parting of the Red Sea, he hears the thumping sounds of approaching helicopters. Clive looks to the sky through his open roof and lifts an arm to wave them onward. "That's right, fellas… Bring on the whirlybirds!"

Drivers steadily peel off to the shoulder and right lanes, as more police join the pursuit. While the whole procession converges to a double-wide line, Clive follows the SUV veering toward the 110 Freeway entrance heading into downtown. Clive reaches over and grabs his cell phone. He flips it open, raises and waves it around, trying to get reception. He looks to the city skyline and grunts, "Figures I wouldn't get any phone connection in the second largest city in America."

The cell phone gets tossed aside, and Clive checks his rearview mirrors, as the chase cars narrow into a single-file line heading toward the city center. Following the SUV, Clive leads the motorcade of police cars over the bridge to downtown, while hovering helicopters observe their approach.

The sight of a news helicopter coming in alongside the LAPD chopper makes Clive nervous, and he mumbles to himself, "The end is near…" His eyes flit to the rearview mirror, and now there are too many vehicles with flashing lights to make an accurate count. They come off the bridge, proceed onto the northbound freeway toward downtown, and pull up to a police roadblock spread out across all five lanes.

At the head of the procession, the white SUV slowly rolls forward to the barricade and stops. Clive comes in a short distance behind and brakes, as the police cars fan out to surround them. As tires roll to a stop, swarms of police officers instantly materialize. SWAT teams carrying automatic rifles encircle the SUV and the sports car, taking position with guns aimed and ready.

Shifting into *park*, Clive shoots his hands skyward through the open top of his car. A police officer using a bullhorn shouts to them both, "Step out of your vehicles and lay face down on the pavement!" After a moment of tense anticipation, the driver's door of the SUV opens. The bullhorn *bleeps* as emergency lights flash in every direction, and draft from the helicopters above swirls the bits of road trash around. Finally, Timothy Gustavo steps out of his vehicle and stands with his arms extended upward. He is instantly surrounded and pounced upon by several officers.

With his hands still raised, Clive watches the suspect struggle, get pressed to the pavement, handcuffed and then searched. Another group of police officers rush in to examine the still-running SUV. Clive starts to lower his hands and murmurs, "Well done, fellas. All in a good day's work…"

All of a sudden, he notices that there is a tight ring of SWAT officers pointing their automatic rifles directly at *him*.

The police bullhorn blares, "Hey... You in the little red car! Keep your hands up, get out of the vehicle, and don't make any sudden moves."

Clive looks up at his raised hands and then down to the door handle. He considers his options, as he looks around at the business ends of the multitude of rifles pointed at him. Thrusting his chin upward to the open rooftop, he pleads, "Don't shoot... I'll give up without a fight."

One of the SWAT members flips the door handle and another one swings open the driver's-side door of the Fiero. Clive, with his hands still held high, slowly eases both legs out and tries to scoot from the seat of his low-profile vehicle. Ahead, a handcuffed Timothy Gustavo is lifted from the pavement and escorted by officers toward an open police car. Clive drags his butt to the edge of the driver's seat and tries to get his feet under himself. Tension mounts, as officers continue to direct their firearms at him. "Get out of the car... Easy now... Lay face down on the pavement!" As instructed, Clive tucks his knees under him and flops forward onto the hot roadway. Instantly, several officers advance on him, jerk his arms behind his back and slap the cuffs on.

Wincing from heavy knees digging into his backside, Clive grunts to the arresting officers. "Hold on there, boys. You've already got the bad guy." They pull him to his feet, usher him to the side of a squad car and read him his rights. Clive looks around at the huge display of law enforcement and the lines of stopped traffic on both sides of the freeway.

Shortly, Clive spots Timothy in the back seat of a nearby squad car, and their gazes connect. Clive offers an impish smile. Speaking to Timothy, but not quite loud enough for him to hear, Clive murmurs, "You needed some special attention? Now you've got it."

Gazing up to the city skyline, Clive takes a deep breath and flexes his wrists in the tight handcuffs. Looking back to the officer who has just finished reading him his rights, he asks, "Hey, is Detective Buckley here by any chance?"

The policeman puts his hand on Clive's shoulder and, in a deadpan tone, asks, "Do you understand your rights?"

"Yes."

"Watch your head, pal." The officer directs him toward the back seat of a police car, but Clive counters with the plea, "Wait… Is Buckley around?"

"He'll be on site soon." The officer ushers him along, adding, "His specific orders are to detain you and keep you away from the media, so sit tight."

Clive breathes a sigh of relief and wiggles the handcuffs behind his back. "These hurt. How about you take them off?"

The officer answer back, "They're not built for comfort." He peers around to peek at Clive's hands, and then offers, "They seem to fit you just fine, and you're still under arrest."

"Really? Why…? I'm the one who single-handedly delivered you *The Santa Monica Sniper*."

The officer grunts, "You delivered a whole lotta mess to clean up, and the media to eat up. Heck, we don't even know if you got the right guy." As the officer's comment sinks in, Clive feels a little less confident about his situation. He looks at the huge police presence and the news helicopters circling above. Suddenly feeling ill, he leans into the squad car, ducks his head, and sits inside.

Chapter 28

The Santa Monica Police Station is buzzing with activity. While Clive sits in a metal chair, his hands still cuffed behind his back, the main hallway is swarming with personnel coming and going. He checks out each of the individuals around him, not recognizing anyone, and no one pays him any notice. Finally, he spots Buckley coming down the hall. Clive mutters, "What the hell, Buckley? I thought you forgot about me."

As he walks past, the detective shakes his head with disgust and gives a wave. "Follow me, Wilts." Struggling to get up without anyone's help, Clive manages to get to his feet and scampers down the hallway after Buckley. When the detective enters a meeting room, Clive stops at the doorway and then hesitantly follows.

Stepping into the unoccupied conference room, Clive looks around and then turns to where Buckley leans on a table. "More questioning? How about you take off the handcuffs? They're starting to chafe."

Buckley stares at Clive and slowly lets a partial grin break through his stern countenance. "Clive... When I said, *We're going to catch this guy, so give us all your leads,* what the hell didn't you understand?"

Clive moves to a much more comfortable, padded chair in the room and eases into it. "Did you check his storage unit? I saw him hide something."

Buckley walks the perimeter of the room and stands behind the chair, so that Clive has to crane his neck to see him. Buckley is silent for a moment. He heaves an irritated breath before responding, "Not only did you give us some ridiculous, half-assed lead... You pursued the suspect without telling us anything first and led a car chase all the way to downtown LA. And, while you were at it, dunder-head, every news helicopter in town got to film it."

When Buckley walks over to the door and closes it with a quiet *click,* Clive chimes in. "On the bright side, I didn't see Channel Seven up there..."

The detective spins on a heel, glares at Clive accusingly. "Dammit, Wilts! They were *all* up there. Not to mention, you revealed important evidence to Catherine McCormick from *Inside California*, which she put up all over the news!"

"Hey, that's not fair... I showed you first, didn't I? Besides, you said you needed a strategic decoy, right?"

As Clive sits uncomfortably with his hands cuffed behind his back, Buckley leans down and gets right in his face. "Wilts, you were on the path to really screw things up." Buckley spins Clive's chair around several times and then goes back to lean on the table.

Dragging both his feet to stop the chair from spinning, Clive optimistically adds, "And *just enough*, so that things turned out right. *Right...*?" He turns to face Buckley and inquires, "Did you check out that storage unit?"

The detective crosses his arms over his chest and nods. "Yes... We found a recently fired weapon in the storage unit."

Surprised, the private investigator breathes a sigh of relief. "Wow, really?"

Buckley continues, "We also developed a roll of film from a camera we found on-site which had incriminating photos from the shooting earlier today."

"Really?!"

"The evidence so far ties him directly to the shootings, but no apparent motive has been found."

"Really...?"

Clive leans forward, trying to relieve the painful pinch of the metal restraints on his wrists. Standing up, Buckley digs in his pocket and produces a tiny handcuff key. He moves over to Clive, while grumbling, "Dammit, Wilts... I hardly have the heart to do this." He unlocks the handcuffs and tosses them onto the conference table.

Finally free, Clive rubs his sore wrists and smirks at the police detective. "Thanks Buckley, I didn't know you had a heart at all."

"We're dropping all charges against you for the freeway pursuit." Clive shakes out his hands and nods approvingly. "That's fair... I appreciate it."

"It sure wasn't what we had in mind for you, Wilts. When you watch the local news, you'll see. Those damn idiots in the media have made a frickin' hero out of you because of what you did."

Delighted, Clive gives Buckley a friendly pat on the shoulder. "I guess they're not *all* that bad."

"Well, once again they saved your ass. Now *you* have to deal with them."

"What do you mean?"

With a sweep of his arm, Buckley motions to the door. "You're free to go, but... There's about a dozen news teams waiting outside to talk to you. And, probably several more at your office *and* at your home..."

The smile drops from Clive's face. "Is my car still impounded in the police lot? Can I slip out the back door?" Arms crossed, the detective cracks a smile and shakes his head. "Nope... We did you the courtesy of parking it out front."

"Out front, huh?"

Buckley nods. "Better put on your game face…"

Clive lowers his chin in a pouty fashion and moves toward the door. "I'll put in a good word for you."

"Keep my name out of it, Hotdog."

~*~

News teams gather outside, as Clive takes the long walk down the crowded hallway toward the front doors. Anxious, he struggles with mixed feelings about facing the media beast. Everyone steps to the side to make way for the reluctant hero. They shake their heads as he passes, knowing what he is about to encounter with the press.

Walking around the front reception desk, he suddenly receives a colossal smack across the seat of his pants. Surprised, he yelps, "Buckley!?"

Instead, Clive turns to see Shannequa, with a big grin on her face, leaning across the counter. "You wish, *Honey-buuuns*! I thought you looked a little serious, Clive-sweetie. You could crack walnuts with that tight ass."

He rubs his tingling backside, winces and grins at the over-friendly clerk. "That was just what I needed, Hot-pants." Clive notices that everyone is watching him. "But, maybe not so hard in front of the children…"

When he turns to look at the media circus gathered outside the windows, Shannequa taps her lengthy fingernails on the desktop and loudly hisses, "Give 'em hell, Muffin-ass."

"Sure thing, Fruit-tits…" Suddenly feeling quite cocky and ready to put on a show, Clive acquires an exaggerated, bow-legged, cowboy walk and marches to the front doors. Shoving them both open wide, like he's leaving a western saloon, he steps out to face the music.

Chapter 29

It's business as usual at the old neighborhood coffee shop. With a coffee and Danish, Clive sits at his usual table, patiently waiting for a chance to lunge at a second-hand newspaper. Suddenly, a folded paper plops down directly in front of him, and he looks up to see Maryanne. She smiles at him playfully. "Hey, Magnum... I bought you a new one."

"Umm... Thanks."

Standing beside an empty chair, she looks at it and raises an eyebrow to the private investigator. "Can I have a seat?" Half-standing, Clive pushes back his own chair and motions her to the empty spot. "Yes, please do."

Maryanne sets her coffee cup down on the table and slides into the seat. She looks to the newspaper, as Clive flushes with awkwardness. Placing her hand on the front page, a slender finger sweeps under the heading. "I thought this one might be a keeper."

Clive peeks at the bold, front-page headline that reads: *Santa Monica Sniper caught by North Hollywood Celebrity Private Eye*. He puts on his game face and does his best to quell his mounting excitement, "Huh? I made the paper, again? Actually, I prefer the term *Private Investigator*."

Taking a sip from her coffee, Maryanne seems genuinely surprised at his lack of enthusiasm on seeing his name and picture on the front page of the daily newspaper. She gives him an admiring look and then comments flirtingly, "Clive Wilts...

133

North Hollywood Private Investigator... Either you're overly modest, or you're the biggest smart-ass around."

He gives her a sly wink and takes a bite of his Danish. With his mouth full, he replies, "All in a day's work..."

~*~

The media crews still crowd in front of the Santa Monica Police Station, waiting for them to give an official statement. Microphone held at the ready, reporter Catherine McCormick, with the lobby entry behind her, stands facing a camera crew. On cue, she gestures to the station's front doors and reports, *"The Santa Monica Sniper was apprehended roughly 24 hours ago. We are still waiting for a Detective Buckley to confirm our findings about the shooter's motive for murder..."*

~*~

Inside Clive's apartment, the television set plays the local news. On-screen, Catherine McCormick reports from the Santa Monica Police Station. She stares into the camera lens and states, *"What would make a seemingly common citizen go on a killing spree of payback and revenge? Was it an ill-timed parking ticket, or was it the unwanted affections of a cold-hearted Meter Maid?"* Pausing for dramatic effect, Catherine steps aside and Clive's shooter photo pops up in the corner of the screen. She adds, *"The story of the Santa Monica Sniper and his twisted life of love, lust and homicide at ten..."*

Clive, on his couch, relaxing with a beer, uses the remote to click the television off. As he lifts his beverage to take a swallow, he hears a female voice call to him from the kitchen. "Do you need another drink, Magnum?"

He swishes the last of his beer and looks over to see Maryanne coming through the door with a fresh one for him. He smiles and winks confidently. "Sure thing, Sweetie-pie..."

The End ...

Civ.et, *n.* 1. A yellowish unctuous substance with a strong musk-like odor, obtained from a pouch in the genital region of civets and used in perfumery. 2. Any of the catlike carnivorous mammals of southern Asia and Africa having glands in the genital region that secrete civet. 3. Any of certain allied or similar animals, as the palm civet.

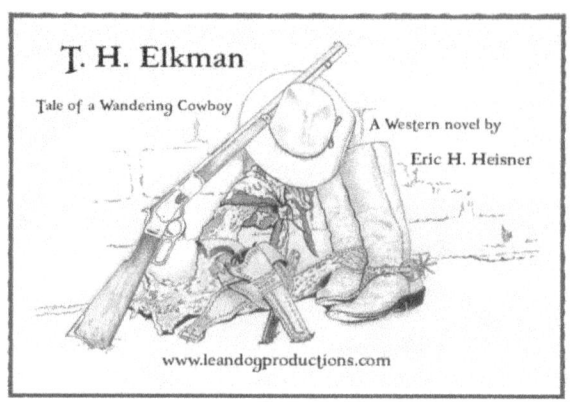

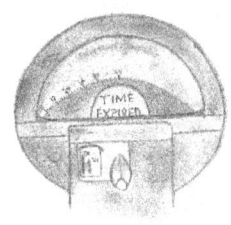

If you enjoyed *Citation for Murder*,
read other stories
by
Eric H. Heisner

www.leandogproductions.com

Eric H. Heisner is an award-winning writer, actor and filmmaker. He is the author of several Western and Adventure novels: *West to Bravo*, *T. H. Elkman*, *Africa Tusk*, *Conch Republic* and *Short Western Tales: Friend of the Devil*. He can be contacted at his website:

www.leandogproductions.com

Adeline Emmalei is a creative artist, student and animal lover. She lives in Austin, Texas.